"I know it's not your place," he told her, and he didn't let his lips curl. Odd that, after everything, she actually made him want to smile. "It's mine."

Elizabeth turned to look at him. "Why am I at your house?"

"Because you're spending the night with me."

He easily heard her sharply indrawn breath.

"Look, Mac," Elizabeth said, "that kiss was a heat-of-the-moment thing. Adrenaline and craziness. It wasn't me offering—offering—"

"To jump into bed with me?" Mac asked as he pulled the car into the garage. He'd moved to that home on the edge of the city just a few weeks before. He'd felt closed in and he'd wanted a new place.

"Right." Her voice was sharp. "I wasn't offering to jump into bed with you."

He killed the engine. "Pity."

"Mac—"

"You're here for your protection." They'd get to the jumping-in-bed and heat-of-the-moment part again later. "In case you missed it, someone is gunning for you."

DECEPTIONS

New York Times Bestselling Author

CYNTHIA EDEN

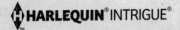

HARLEQUIN® INTRIGUE®

Thank you, THANK YOU to all of the
amazing Harlequin Intrigue readers out there! I so appreciate you
taking the time to read about the McGuire family!

ISBN-13: 978-0-373-69897-4

Deceptions

Copyright © 2016 by Cindy Roussos

Recycling programs
for this product may
not exist in your area.

Printed in U.S.A.

www.Harlequin.com

Cynthia Eden, a *New York Times* bestselling author, writes tales of romantic suspense and paranormal romance. Her books have received starred reviews from *Publishers Weekly*, and she has received a RITA® Award nomination for best romantic suspense novel. Cynthia lives in the Deep South, loves horror movies and has an addiction to chocolate. More information about Cynthia may be found at cynthiaeden.com, or you can follow her on Twitter, @cynthiaeden.

Books by Cynthia Eden

Harlequin Intrigue

The Battling McGuire Boys

Confessions
Secrets
Suspicions
Reckonings
Deceptions

Shadow Agents

Alpha One
Guardian Ranger
Sharpshooter
Glitter and Gunfire

Shadow Agents: Guts and Glory

Undercover Captor
The Girl Next Door
Evidence of Passion
Way of the Shadows

Visit the Author Profile page at Harlequin.com for more titles.

CAST OF CHARACTERS

Elizabeth Snow—This by-the-book librarian is hiding a troubled past and keeping dark secrets from the rest of the world. Elizabeth let her wild side out once before—with deadly consequences—and she's now determined to play things safe. But when her past comes back to haunt her, only Mackenzie "Mac" McGuire can keep her safe. Too bad Mac is exactly the kind of man she should never want—dangerous and far too *wild*.

Mac McGuire—Mac is well used to danger, and the former Delta Force member loves nothing more than to lose himself in the adrenaline rush of battle. Known as the wildest McGuire brother, he has spent plenty of years raising hell. But when danger stalks Elizabeth, everything changes for Mac. *She* is his priority, and to keep her safe, he will take any risk and fight any threat that comes her way.

Sullivan McGuire—Sullivan has been keeping secrets from his family, but he is tired of carrying his pain in silence. When a new case brings him face-to-face with the woman he loved and lost so long ago, even he can't predict the desperate turn his life will take.

Steve Yeldon—A reporter who won't rest until he uncovers the truth, Steve has put a dangerous target on his back. He wants to help Elizabeth, but when a killer comes gunning for him, Steve may not even be able to help himself.

Melinda Chafer—Detective Chafer believes in fighting for truth and justice, even if there are some guys at Internal Affairs who might think otherwise. Melinda knows that she can prove herself, but when she gets drawn into the web of Elizabeth's tangled past, she learns that even a good cop can be tempted to walk away from the law.

Chapter One

She should have been alone.

Elizabeth Snow had the late shift at the small library nestled on the outskirts of Austin, Texas. She was the one scheduled to close and secure the facility. She *should* have been the only one there.

So why had she just heard the faint pad of footsteps coming from the back?

Elizabeth froze a few feet from the library's exit. Her purse was slung over her shoulder, and her fingers had a pretty strong death grip on the strap. Shadows loomed from the heavy shelves of books, seeming to reach for her.

Normally, the library was a haven for her. So safe. So secure. But...

It was late. Those shadows were thick and—

She heard a very distinct *thud*. As if a book had just fallen off a shelf. Or been knocked off. Elizabeth swallowed and called out, "Is someone there? The library is closed now. You need to leave." She tried to use her firmest voice.

Silence.

Maybe her imagination was just a little too active.

She *had* spent the last weekend watching a horror marathon on TV. Perhaps she was—

Thud. Okay, that definitely had sounded like a book falling to the floor. *Someone is playing with me.*

They'd never had any kind of security issue before. Sure, sometimes folks fell asleep among the library shelves, curled up at one of the tables, and those people would miss the announcements about closing time. But when she did her final walk-through, she gently woke them up and sent them on their way.

She'd done her walk-through a few minutes before and had found no stragglers.

"The library is closed!" She took a tentative step back toward her desk.

"Elizabeth..."

It was a whisper, raspy and low and male, and it had her tensing.

"Who's there?" Elizabeth demanded, voice rising. "This isn't funny. I'll call security!" A total lie. There was no security at the library. Not then, anyway.

"Been...waiting..."

His voice sounded closer.

No, this could not be happening to her. "Stop it!" Elizabeth called. "Just—"

Someone banged on the door, a hard knock that had her yelling—screaming—in surprise and whirling toward the glass doors.

A tall man stood at the main entrance. His shoulders were wide, almost ridiculously so, and his powerful chest was obviously muscled. She recognized him on sight—it was rather hard to forget a man like him—and Elizabeth normally would have just paused to admire the very fine sight of MacKenzie "Mac" McGuire, but right then—

She flew toward the door. Her breath sawed in and out of her lungs, and her heart raced as her fingers fumbled to disengage the lock.

Mac held up his book, a thriller she'd picked out for him during his last visit to the library. "Sorry to come in so late," he said, his voice that deep, rolling rumble that she secretly adored. "But I saw the light on and I figured you'd be—"

She grabbed him. His book tumbled to the floor. "Someone is in here."

Mac's green eyes narrowed on her. His face—a dangerously handsome face that *maybe* she fantasized a bit about—hardened. "What?"

She kept one hand on him and pointed behind her with the other. "I heard him. He's back there, calling my name! I don't—"

He pushed her behind him and immediately started stalking toward the shelves. She knew that Mac—like his brothers—had spent time in the military. According to the gossip she'd picked up, Mac was ex-Delta Force, as tough as they came. As he moved forward with the slow, steady stride of a predator, she could practically feel the battle-ready tension pouring off him.

She crept behind him, trying to move as softly as he did, but totally failing as her purse and keys jingled and jangled with her steps. Mac paused and glanced back at her, frowning.

She pointed to the left. "There," Elizabeth mouthed. "He came from—"

Glass shattered. Only the sound hadn't come from the left. It had come from the right. Mac took off running. She grabbed the first weapon she saw on her desk and rushed after him. Her high heels were slowing her down so she just kicked them off. She rounded the shelves, twisted around the library cart and then she—

Ran into Mac.

Their bodies collided with a hard impact and before she could send them both hurtling to the floor, Mac's hands flew up and wrapped around her. He steadied them both, holding her easily. She'd never been so close to him before. Never fully appreciated just how strong the guy was or how good he smelled and—

"He's getting away."

Oh, yes, right. She tried to back up.

"A stapler?" Mac muttered. "What the hell?"

She glanced at her left hand and the weapon she'd grabbed moments before. The stapler was pretty solid. It could do some damage if used properly.

But Mac didn't give her time to reply. He whirled toward the window. Whoever the mystery man had been, he'd shattered the glass as he made his getaway. Mac took a second to punch out more of the glass that jutted out from the window, and then he leaped out into the night. He ran forward, vanishing, and she peered out the window, staring after him as she held that stapler tight. An alarm began to beep. Finally, the library's alarm had kicked in. It *should* have sounded as soon as the glass broke.

She leaned even closer to the window, straining to see Mac. It was so dark out there. Was he okay? What if he'd just run straight into an ambush of some kind? The fingers of her right hand brushed aside the glass.

A car's revving engine vibrated in the night. There

was a flash of headlights, and that vibrating engine grew louder as the vehicle raced away.

Someone was in here, calling my name. Someone had been stalking her.

Been waiting... His whisper drifted through her mind once again. She hated the fear that filled her. A fear that reminded her—*no matter how far you run, there are some things you can't escape.*

"Mac?" Elizabeth called as the alarm kept beeping. The cops would arrive soon. The alarm company would contact them, but what good would they do? That car—and the man who'd been in the library—were long gone now.

"Mac?" His name was louder this time as she peered into the darkness. Where had he gone? What if that nut in the car had hurt him? Sure, she got that Mac was supposed to be some kind of super tough guy, but even tough guys didn't win in fights with moving vehicles. What if he'd been hit; what if—

"Elizabeth."

She whirled and swung the stapler at him.

Sighing, Mac caught her wrist in his hand. The move was incredibly fast. Scary fast. Super reflex fast. Then, keeping his right hand around hers, his left removed the stapler and tossed it aside. "He's gone."

And she was about to jump out of her skin. "You scared me to death!" Elizabeth accused him. "What were you thinking?"

His dark brows shot up. "I called your name three times. The alarm is so loud you just didn't hear me."

She blinked. "Oh. Right."

"The system is set up to alert the cops, isn't it?" He

was still holding her hand. She could feel the roughness of calluses on his fingertips.

"It is," Elizabeth said. She had to look back over her shoulder, peering out that window into the darkness once more.

"They'll check the scene, but he's long gone. I didn't see a tag on the car. Didn't see much of anything because the joker waited and tried to blind me with his bright lights."

She remembered the flash of light that had burst into the darkness.

"Are you okay?" Mac asked her.

And…his fingers were sliding lightly against the inside of her wrist. The touch was almost a caress, and it made her nervous. Edgy. But then again, Mac usually made her feel that way.

He'd started coming into the library a few weeks ago. The first time she'd looked up and seen him standing on the opposite side of the checkout counter, her jaw had dropped. *Sexy.* That was the only word for Mac, with his dark hair, that hard jaw, his sensual lips and—

Sirens.

Sirens were screaming outside. The cops were responding way faster than she'd anticipated.

"Elizabeth," Mac pushed. "Are you okay?"

She forced herself to smile. "Fine. I'm glad you were here." That was probably one of the most honest things she'd said in months. If he hadn't shown up, just what would she have done?

Mac didn't release her. "Do you have any enemies, Elizabeth?"

She kept her smile in place. "I'm a librarian. I try really hard not to make too many people angry."

He kept staring at her. No humor softened his face. Right. This wasn't the time for humor.

She let her smile vanish. "Thank you." Her voice was softer. The sirens were louder. "I owe you a serious debt of gratitude."

He let her go. "I'll collect on that debt."

What?

"Later. For now, let's go meet the cops before some uniform comes in here with guns blazing." He steered her toward the main door. "Watch out for the glass."

It crunched beneath their feet.

"HE DROPPED THE knife when he was running." Mac hadn't wanted to tell Elizabeth that fact; at least, not right away. He just hadn't wanted to scare her too much.

But the cops had finished their sweep in the library, and now they were searching the road—and the exact spot where the would-be attacker had fled.

"There," Mac said, pointing. "I didn't touch it in case there were prints left behind."

"A knife?" Elizabeth said, her normally husky, sexy voice turning into a sharp cry of fear. "What? He had a *knife*?"

Yes, and that fact had fury surging inside Mac. The cops hadn't seemed overly concerned when they'd first appeared on the scene. He'd heard them muttering about kids and pranks. And he'd known they needed to get to the knife ASAP.

One bent and carefully inspected the knife. "A switchblade," he said, and he glanced up at Mac. "You *sure* the guy dropped it? I mean, it's really dark out here and—"

"He dropped it," Mac said flatly. "So get it checked

for prints." When some bozo hid in a vacant library, waiting with a *knife*, the cops should know that meant trouble.

From the corner of his eye, Mac saw Elizabeth take a step back. Her hand was near her mouth and, if there'd been more light, he was sure he would have seen horror reflected in her warm brown eyes.

Elizabeth Snow.

He remembered the first time he'd seen the new librarian. He'd been there to study the newspaper archives, looking for any stories that might have hit when his mother first came to town, so long ago. Those records hadn't been digitized, but there were microfiche copies in the library. It had been his first venture into old-school research.

And his first glimpse of Elizabeth.

Her hair had been loose around her shoulders, a dark curtain that framed her heart-shaped face. She'd been laughing when she turned toward him, but as soon as she glanced into his eyes, her laughter had stopped.

Don't stop. His immediate thought. Because he'd liked the sound of her laughter.

Red had stained her high cheekbones, and her full lips had still been curved into a smile when she asked if she could help him.

In so many ways, so many.

The police lights were flashing around them, and he saw her trembling hand tucking her hair behind her ear. "He came after me with a knife?"

The uniforms shared a glance. "We don't know exactly what his intentions were, ma'am," one said carefully. "Maybe the guy thought he could rob you, possibly get some money from the cash register inside."

"There *is* no cash inside. We charge for overdue books, that's it. There's not enough money in there worth stealing." Her arms wrapped around her stomach. "And he called my name."

Which meant, in Mac's book, that the attack had definitely been personal. He edged closer to Elizabeth. Something was going on here, something that he was missing. When he'd asked her if she had any enemies, her voice had hitched a bit when she replied.

Lie.

So he couldn't help but wonder: Just what sort of enemies would a sweet librarian have? And Elizabeth was sweet. She smelled like cinnamon, and he pretty much wanted to damn well gobble her up. He'd seen her reading to the kids, leading them in story-time dances. He'd seen her *too much.*

Hell... *I'm the one turning into a stalker.*

"And why were you here, Mr. McGuire?" one of the cops asked as if reading his thoughts.

"I—"

"He was turning in a book," Elizabeth said quickly. "And I am so very glad that he was."

Mac shrugged. "It was overdue." A total lie. He'd just wanted to see her.

"I'll waive that fine," Elizabeth said, for some reason choosing to go along with his story as her fingers brushed his shoulder. Mac couldn't help it—he tensed at her touch. It seemed as if an electric current shot right through him. There was just something about Elizabeth...

Her hand dropped.

She backed away.

Something about her, but the woman is not interested

in me. He'd tried to ask her out before. A time or two. Or four. She'd shot him down every time.

He guessed that a rough and ready ex-Delta Force member wasn't her idea of proper date material. Too bad. She should know that opposites could definitely attract.

"I called the library's director," Elizabeth said. "She's coming to make sure the window is secured. She said the alarm team would be here soon, too."

He glanced to the left. As if on cue, a blue SUV was pulling up. When the interior lights flashed on, he recognized the woman inside—Cathy Waite, the director.

"I have to talk with her," Elizabeth said as she hurried off.

Mac didn't follow her. Instead, he stepped closer to the cops. "When a man stalks a woman in a building like this, with a knife at the ready, that's serious damn trouble."

"W-we'll run that knife—"

"He only fled when he heard me. That jerk had plans tonight. He was going to hurt her." His hands clenched into fists. "You need to find that guy before he strikes again." *Before I get to him first.*

Mac glanced over his shoulder at Elizabeth. She and Cathy were talking as a service truck pulled up.

"They can't start working on that window yet," one of the cops said when he spied the truck. "We're not done with our investigation!" Then he was rushing forward.

Mac's gaze slid to Elizabeth. She was rubbing her arms again, as if she was cold. He shrugged out of his jacket and headed toward her. When he put the jacket around her shoulders, she jumped a bit. Hell, he had to *stop* scaring her. Mac was used to moving silently, and sometimes he forgot how disconcerting that could be for people.

Her fingers curled around the jacket. "Thank you." The damn thing swallowed her delicate frame. He glanced down and saw that she'd put her shoes back on. Earlier, she'd kicked them off and he'd seen her toes, painted a bright fire-engine red. The cops had returned the shoes to her.

"You should go," Elizabeth said with a little nod. "The cops are here, Cathy's here...we have to get things secured. You just... You've already gone above and beyond in your library-patron duty."

"I don't mind hanging around," Mac said, trying to sound casual.

The flashing lights swirled around them. Elizabeth stepped a bit closer to him. Sweet cinnamon wrapped around him. "You don't have to stay," Elizabeth said softly. "But thank you for playing hero." Then she started to take off his jacket.

He lifted his hand, stopping her. "Keep it. I've got others." And he didn't want her cold.

She flashed him a smile. "Like I said, I owe you, Mac."

"Then maybe you can repay that debt by having a drink with me." The words hung between them.

She bit her lip. A bad move because he found it sexy. He wanted to touch that lip, lick it. Maybe bite it. Not too hard, of course. What would his sweet librarian do then?

"I don't think we'd be a good idea," Elizabeth said.

Shot down for the fifth time. He was a man who could take a hint. "Why not?" He touched her cheek and saw the quick breath that she took. Saw the tremble that shook her. "I know you feel it, too." *It*. That heady awareness between them. The connection that said they'd pretty much ignite together.

"I do." She tipped back her head to stare up at him. "But I don't think I can handle what you'd want from me."

"I bet you could."

"I heard the stories about you." Her voice had dropped to a whisper. "You're all about danger. Adrenaline." Elizabeth shook her head. "That life isn't for me. I can't do that."

He nodded. "I wasn't asking you to head out on a mission with me. I was just talking about a drink."

She laughed. Hell, he really liked that laugh. And for her to be able to laugh there, after everything that had happened...

"I do owe you, Mac," Elizabeth said. "So I think I'd like that drink date." She hesitated. "I just, I can't offer more than that. You need to know that going in."

"Understood." He knew how to be a gentleman, though he was sure plenty of people would disagree. The rough and ready McGuire brothers had gotten a pretty strong reputation over the years, and gossip did like to fly.

He didn't particularly care what the gossips thought. But Mac *did* care about what Elizabeth thought.

She hurried to join Cathy once more. Mac turned toward his car. He'd taken just a few steps when he stopped and glanced back at the now well-lit library.

What if the guy comes back?

MAC WAS A temptation she didn't need. Elizabeth slammed her car door and hurried up the sidewalk to her house. She should be steering clear of the guy and everything that he represented. Instead, she'd agreed to drinks.

And she wanted more.

There was something between them—lust. Desire. She got that. She tried to play it cool around him, but a very large part of her wanted to jump the man on sight.

Her heels clicked over her sidewalk as she hurried home. She glanced around, a bit nervous, but her neighborhood was safe. There were plenty of dogs close by. Plenty of helpful, wonderfully nosy folks like her neighbor Judy Lee, who kept a watch on things.

Her key slid into the lock. She should cancel that drink date with Mac. Though, technically, they hadn't planned a date. They'd just said they would have drinks. Sometime. Somewhere. And she would *not* jump him.

She most definitely would *not* let her wild side out with Mac, even though he did tempt her. He made her want things…excitement, passion…things that could be dangerous.

As dangerous as he is.

She went into her house. Flipped on the light. And—

Her phone rang.

Fumbling, Elizabeth pulled out the phone and frowned at the screen. She didn't recognize the number that appeared there. A number, no name.

Who could be calling her at this hour? She rarely ever gave out her own number. She hadn't even given it to Mac. But she *had* given it to the police. Maybe they'd caught the guy already! She kicked the door shut with her foot, flipped the lock and answered, "This is Elizabeth—"

"Beth."

Ice poured through her veins.

"I know what he's after, Beth. I can help you."

"Who is this?" She put her back to the door, and her tight grip probably came close to splintering her phone.

"We both found you, but we can stop him."

"Who is this?" Elizabeth demanded again as fear pulsed through her. First the attack, now this guy... *Why is this happening?*

"Meet me now. Before it's too late."

"Too late for what?" Elizabeth turned and peered through her blinds. Had a car just glided to a stop in front of Ms. Lee's? It was so dark under that big tree, it was hard to tell for certain, but a car *could* be there. "I think you've got the wrong woman."

"I was there, in Colorado, Beth." His voice sounded vaguely familiar. "I want to help you."

The guy at the library had wanted to hurt her. "What you need to do is leave me alone," she said, injecting a note of steel into her voice. "Stay away from me."

"You're in danger!"

"Are you threatening me?" She was pretty sure that she'd just seen a shadow move out there beneath the tree. Her knees were knocking together.

"I'm trying to help you!"

Right. Was she supposed to foolishly believe that? The guy wouldn't even tell her who he was!

"Look, I couldn't let the past go. I was asking questions, talking too much—I showed my hand too soon."

Okay, now she was just lost.

"Because of that, we're both in danger."

She still had on Mac's jacket, but a chill skated down her spine.

"I know I'm being hunted, and so are you. Meet me," he said, his voice still oddly familiar, but she couldn't quite place it. She usually had a knack for remembering voices. "Now. I'm close to a bar on Avers Street. A place called Rustic. Meet me in the alley outside."

Sure. Because she had a death wish. She'd just skip right into a dark alley with a stranger who called her the same night that she'd nearly been attacked.

"I can help you stop him." His voice deepened. "I know what happened before, okay? I was there. I reported on it."

Reported—with that one word, his voice clicked, and she had a flash in her mind of a man—tall, a little thin, with sandy-blond hair and blue eyes that she'd actually thought held compassion.

But that had been a lifetime ago. Elizabeth had been a different person back then.

"You have me confused with someone else," she said.

"Beth, no, don't hang up." His breath heaved out in a sigh that filled the phone. "You came to Texas because of what happened, didn't you? Because this was his home? Part of you has to be looking for closure. I want that closure, too! I figured it out—everything. Come see me and we can stop— Ah!"

His words ended on a sharp cry. A cry of pain?

"Hello?" Elizabeth said. "Are you okay?"

Click. Silence. The call had ended.

"Hello?" She hit the call-back button but the line just rang and rang. After a few moments voice mail picked up.

This is Steve Yeldon. If you've got a story for me, leave a message. Otherwise...why are you calling me?

Steve Yeldon. That name was straight from her past. Elizabeth lowered the phone and stared at the screen. She remembered that reporter. He'd been young, only a few years older than she was. He hadn't attacked her, not the way so many others had. He'd kept asking for her side of the story.

She hadn't wanted to talk.

But that had been years ago.

Her finger slipped over her phone's screen one more time. His last cry had sent goose bumps rising over her arms and had dread lodging in her heart. She tried calling back once more, needing to actually talk to him again and have Steve tell her that he'd just been disconnected, that everything was fine—

Someone answered the phone. She could hear the rush of breath.

"Hello?" Elizabeth said. "Is this Steve Yeldon?"

The rush of breath came over the line again.

"Steve, look, I don't want—"

"Steve can't talk right now."

The low, raspy voice sent more shivers over her. "Who is this?"

"I'll see you soon, Elizabeth."

A distinct click filled her ears as fear knotted her stomach.

Her first instinct was to call the cops, to get to that alley but—

The cops didn't believe me before. Not back when she'd first met Steve Yeldon. Her past with the cops was twisted and dark. She didn't turn to them these days. Mostly because she didn't trust them to help her.

But Steve needs help.

And she…she was the only one who could help him.

Elizabeth straightened her shoulders and grabbed for her car keys.

Chapter Two

Mac didn't even know what the hell he was doing. He shouldn't have followed Elizabeth back to her house. He definitely shouldn't be lurking outside like some kind of stalker.

He'd just been worried. As if that made his tailing routine right. He raked a hand through his hair. The woman was home, safe and sound, so he should leave. Right then and *not* go up to her door. But…something kept nagging at him…

She has enemies. She's keeping them secret.

He turned back toward his car. He'd talk to her tomorrow. Like a normal person. Like—

Elizabeth ran out of her house. *Ran.*

"Hey—" Mac called.

She jumped into her car, reversed with a squeal of her tires and nearly took out her mailbox. Her vehicle shot past him, fishtailing a bit, but he was already jumping in his own ride. He knew something was wrong. A person only drove that fast and hard when there was serious danger at play.

Elizabeth had told him that she didn't like danger.

He cranked his car and headed after her. He followed Elizabeth's car as she cut toward Austin, going to the downtown area and hitting the streets that were filled with clubs. He wouldn't have pegged Elizabeth for the club type, but he'd been wrong about people before. Some of those mistakes had nearly proved fatal for him and his brothers.

Elizabeth pulled into a public parking lot. She hadn't seemed to notice that he was tailing her. He figured she'd been driving too fast to notice. His car idled by the curb. He didn't see any threats around there. When he lowered his car window, the beat of music filled the air, and laughter floated in the wind.

Time to stop seeing trouble everywhere. She's just hitting a club. Going for a drink, with someone else.

She'd sure been in an awful big hurry for that drink.

Elizabeth headed toward Rustic, a bar he recognized. Not the worst place, but not the best, either.

Shaking his head, Mac—

Elizabeth ran into the alley. The alley, not the bar. Mac straightened in his seat. What the hell was she doing?

Leave. I should leave. No one is threatening her.

The alley entrance waited, and Elizabeth had vanished.

SOMETIMES YOU KNEW when you were making a bad mistake. When she stepped into that alley, Elizabeth knew she should turn around. She should get the heck out of there as fast as her feet could carry her.

It was fear that stopped her from turning around and fleeing. She was terribly afraid that something had happened to Steve Yeldon. That last gasp kept replaying in her head.

As far as alleys went, she figured this was a relatively nice one. The smell was manageable—mostly the scent of garbage and cheap alcohol permeated the space. There were a few garbage bins around the area—big green metal monsters. The alley was dim, and the only lights seemed to be coming from the nearby buildings.

She inched forward, trying to see in the shadows behind some of those big bins. "Steve? Um, Steve Yeldon? Are you here?" Elizabeth took a few more steps into that darkness. He didn't answer her, so she pulled out her phone and dialed his number again.

There were a few moments of tense silence and then…

Ringing. Very distinct ringing that seemed to be coming from directly behind the bin to the left.

She lowered the phone. "Steve?"

There was the faintest rustle then. Like clothing that had brushed against something.

"Steve? Are you hurt?" She risked another step toward the big bin. Maybe it was Steve over there or… maybe it was that scary guy who'd taunted her.

Trying to be ready, she yanked her pepper spray out of her purse. Then she leaped to the side of that garbage bin, ready to attack.

But you didn't attack the dead. One look, and Elizabeth knew she was staring at a dead man. His body was slumped, twisted, too still. And even in that dim light, she could see the dark pool beneath his body. Her fingers swiped over her phone, and she turned on her flashlight app. The light from her phone flooded the scene and revealed Steve's face. A little older now, a little leaner and very definitely dead.

Blood was everywhere. So much blood. She backed

away, stumbling a bit. She was still holding her phone and her pepper spray and—

A rat crawled from beneath the garbage bin and raced past Steve's body. She screamed, the cry breaking from her even as she realized that rat must have caused the strange rustling sound she'd heard before. It must have been him and—

"Got you."

Hard arms wrapped around Elizabeth and yanked her back. The phone fell from her fingers but it didn't matter. What mattered was her pepper spray. His arms were a fierce band around her stomach, and he had her lifted up so that her legs dangled. She couldn't kick back at him, but she sure tried. She twisted her body, flipped her hand around and she closed her own eyes as she shot that pepper spray back at him.

He yelled, a guttural cry, and released her. Elizabeth hit the cement, scraping her hands and finding herself way too close to a dead body.

"Elizabeth!" Her head jerked up at that roar. It was a cry that wasn't coming from her attacker. Instead, that fierce bellow had come from the front of the alley. She could see the outline of a man—tall, strong—and he was rushing forward.

Her attacker fled, his footsteps pounding by her. She pushed up to her feet, ignoring the sting on her hands and knees as Mac hurried toward her. He locked his arms around her and pulled her close. "Elizabeth! Are you okay?"

Yes. No. Mostly. She wasn't the dead one, so that was something. "He killed Steve."

"What? Who the hell is Steve?"

She pointed to the body.

Mac swore.

She pulled from his arms and started running after her attacker. "We have to stop him!" They couldn't let a killer just escape.

Mac raced at her side. There was a sharp turn up ahead, and then the alley opened up on another street. When they shot out of that alley exit, cars zipped by them, and a shrill honk filled the air. Mac's hand wrapped around her waist, and he dragged her back when she was about to rush right into the traffic.

"Elizabeth, stop!" Mac ordered. "You have to be careful!"

She yanked free of him. "We have to hurry and find the guy!" She whirled around, searching the area. There were plenty of cars, more clubs and no sign of a man running away. No man with Steve's blood on him and tears streaming down his cheeks.

The pepper spray would make the attacker's eyes water. His face would be red. And since he'd stabbed Steve, he should be covered in blood.

But everyone on that street looked so normal.

She backed up and bumped into Mac. "Where is he?" He couldn't get away. He'd killed that reporter. And if they didn't find him…

I think he'll kill me, too.

It was nearing dawn. Most people in Austin were just getting ready to start a new day. Mac was in the office of McGuire Securities, but he wasn't about to start his day.

He was still ending the night from hell.

He stared across his desk at Elizabeth. Her shoulders were hunched. Her skin was too pale. She was too quiet.

He'd stayed with her while the cops were called to that alley. He'd watched her retreat into a shell. He'd listened as she'd too carefully answered the questions from the detective who'd been lead at the scene.

I found the body. He was just...just lying there. His attacker grabbed me. No, I didn't see his face. No, I don't know anything about the victim. I can't help you.

"Elizabeth." He said her name now, deliberately, trying to pull her back to him. During the drive to the office, she'd sat in the passenger seat of his car, but she'd seemed a million miles away.

She still seemed that far away. And she hadn't looked up at his call.

Mac rose from his chair and walked around his desk. He leaned over her and put his hands on her shoulders. "Elizabeth."

She jumped and her eyes—so deep and dark—focused on his. He wondered if she might be in shock. It wasn't every day that a person stumbled onto a murder scene.

Though he wasn't exactly convinced that she'd just *stumbled* onto it.

"I should go home," Elizabeth said, her voice a bit hoarse. "I don't know why I even came here with you."

He knew. Because she'd been dazed and lost in her own thoughts. The woman had been busy hiding her own secrets. "You need my help."

A furrow appeared between her brows.

"I backed you up tonight," he said, keeping his voice gentle for her, "even though I knew you were lying to the cops."

She immediately tried to rise, but he carefully pushed her back into the chair.

"I don't know what you're talking about." Now Elizabeth was glaring at him. "Get your hands off me."

Fine. He pulled his hands back, but he stayed close. "You knew that dead man. You told the cops you didn't, but I heard you say 'He killed Steve.' And you flew out of your house like the place was on fire. You raced to that alley—you *knew* he was in there."

She rose. This time he didn't stop her. He also didn't back up. Their bodies brushed. "You followed me," Elizabeth accused.

"Guilty." He just shrugged.

"Why? You can't just…follow people."

"I'm a PI. I follow lots of people."

She licked her lips. He shouldn't have focused so much on the delectable little flash of her tongue, not with everything else going on, but he did.

"Why were you following me?" She edged back a bit.

"Because I was worried about you. I wanted you *safe.*"

She shook her head. "You don't know me." Elizabeth headed for the door. "I don't even know what I was thinking! I just left my car down there and—"

"You were thinking you wanted to get away. You were thinking that you could be next, and in case anyone might be watching, you didn't want that jerk to see you leaving alone." Well, that last one had certainly been his intent. It wasn't his first murder, not even close. He knew killers. Sometimes he thought he knew them too well. And if the killer had been lingering in the crowd, hiding close by, he hadn't wanted the guy to think that Elizabeth would be an easy target.

Her shoulders stiffened as Elizabeth glanced over at him.

"Someone is after you," Mac said.

She didn't speak.

"Dammit, I can help you! That's what we do here at McGuire Securities. We investigate. We protect. You knew that guy was dead in the alley and—"

"I hoped he wasn't."

She was talking to him. Hell, yes. Now they were making some progress.

Elizabeth turned to face him. She ran a hand through her hair, tousling the thick mane. "I don't trust you."

He almost smiled. "I don't trust you, either." He wanted her, no doubt about that. But as far as trusting her? He'd just seen the woman lie to cops. That didn't exactly inspire undying trust in him.

"I hadn't seen or heard from Steve Yeldon in years. But as soon as I got home tonight, he called me."

He stepped toward her. "If it had been years, then how'd he get your number?"

"He was a reporter! Don't they have sources?" She waved that away. "He called me and said that we needed to meet. He told me to come to that alley. Said we had to talk."

He waited, but Elizabeth didn't tell him anything else. Mac sighed. "What did he want to talk with you about?"

"How should I know?" Her gaze cut away from his. "I've been here for about three months now. I mind my own business. I don't get involved in any drama or dangerous situations and—"

He laughed. Mac just couldn't help it.

Her cheeks reddened.

"You were attacked in your library. You ran into a dark alley and found a dead man." He huffed out a breath. "That actually does count as dangerous. Two dangerous situations."

She looked away, her gaze sliding to his window. Soon the rising sun would fill that window.

"Why did he want to talk with you?" Mac pressed again.

"I don't know." She sounded sincere. "Steve said that we could stop *him*. I don't know who that mysterious *him* is or why we'd want to stop him."

"If you didn't know, then why did you go to the alley?"

Her gaze fell.

A dark suspicion swept over him. "Elizabeth?"

"Because Steve gasped on the phone." Her gaze rose once more and met his. Sadness was in her dark stare. "There was pain in that sound. Fear. After that gasp, he didn't say another word to me. The line went dead."

Probably because Steve had been dead.

"I called back and someone else answered. He said… he said, 'Steve can't talk right now.'"

"What?" Shock rippled through him. "You talked to the killer? You didn't mention that to the cops!"

She flinched. "That wasn't all he said."

This couldn't get worse.

"He told me, 'I'll see you soon, Elizabeth.'"

He couldn't help it. He grabbed her. His fingers curled around her shoulders as he trapped her between his body and the door. "The jerk threatened you, and you didn't mention this phone call to the cops? Why the hell not?"

She stared up at him, the fear plain to see in her eyes. "You know the incident at the library is connected to this," he said. "You have to know it." Coincidences that big never happened.

Elizabeth nodded.

"Why won't you go to the cops? Why won't you tell them—"

"Cops didn't believe me before. I don't have the best experience with them."

Before? Just how many secrets was the pretty librarian keeping from him?

"This isn't your problem," she said, swallowing. "I'm not your problem."

Yes, you are. "Hire me."

"I—I don't have the money—"

"We can work out a deal." He didn't care about her money. He cared about her safety. Cared about getting rid of the fear in her eyes. "You need protection. You need help. Baby, you need me."

"Did you…did you just call me *baby*?"

He had. A slip. Mac cleared his throat. "A killer has you in his sights. That's plain to see. You won't let the cops help you, then let me help you. You know what McGuire Securities can do."

"I've heard some stories about your family," she allowed.

Okay, that might not be the best thing. The stories that circulated about him and his brothers—those stories weren't always the warm and cuddly sort. More like the type to give a person nightmares. "You want us on your side. Whatever is going on here, do you really want to face it alone?"

Her gaze lowered, and her long, dark lashes fell against her cheeks. He was aware right then of just how close he was to her. Their bodies brushed. His hands were still curved around her shoulders. He'd been secretly fantasizing about the woman for weeks—and now she was in his grasp.

Too bad it had taken danger and death to bring them together.

"Twenty-four hours," he threw out, because he wasn't going to let her leave that office without help. "Give me twenty-four hours to figure out what's happening and to see if we can stop the creep out there."

Her lashes lifted. "You're going to take me back to the cops, aren't you?"

Unfortunately, he was. Not that he trusted cops one hundred percent, either, not with his family's track record, but... "You have to tell them about that phone call. Tell them what the guy said to you. If you don't, you're obstructing justice. You're just making it harder for them to find the bastard we're after." He got it— she didn't trust cops, but they didn't have an option, not now. "I'll stay with you, every minute. And then..."

"Then you want your twenty-four hours."

He nodded. "Then I want you to start telling me some of the secrets you carry, and I want you to trust me and my family to keep you safe *and* to track down that killer."

The drumming of his heartbeat filled his ears. Twenty-four hours. That wasn't all he wanted, not by a long shot. But it was a start. Step one.

"Okay..."

Satisfaction burned through him.

"But I have to pay you. Some way, I'll pay you."

"We'll get to payment later. For now we have a detective who we need to call."

"Is there anything else?" the blonde detective asked Elizabeth, her light blue eyes holding more than a hint of suspicion. "Because if the caller said anything else to you…"

"He didn't," Elizabeth told her quickly. The last hour had been spent in Mac's office while Detective Melinda Chafer asked question after question. *At least she didn't make me go to the station.*

And had Mac been right before? Was it technically obstruction since the cops at the scene of the murder had never asked Elizabeth about the phone call? She didn't think so, not exactly, but…

I've messed up. I know it. Fear made me just want to keep my head down and run. But keeping her head down and running wasn't an MO that she could follow this time.

Or maybe she was just tired of running.

"What's your connection to Steve Yeldon?" Melinda asked. "Why did he call you?"

Right. Well, if she was going to talk then there was no sense holding back now. She was far too aware of Mac's heavy gaze on her.

"Eight years ago I was…my boyfriend was killed. Nate Daniels. His name was Nate." She didn't like to think of Nate, because it hurt too much. "The cops never found his killer." *Tell her. Just say it.* "And a lot of people in that area, they thought that maybe I was the killer."

From the corner of her eye, she saw Mac stiffen.

Right. And *this* was why she hadn't told the cops about her connection to Steve Yeldon right away. One of the reasons, anyway. She hated it when people looked at her with suspicion.

"Did you kill him?" Melinda asked with no inflection in her voice.

"No." *Keep it simple.* "Steve was one of the few people who didn't think I was guilty. And for a while, I know he was doing some big exposés, trying to find the *real* killer."

Melinda's gaze was still on her. "Was that real killer ever found?"

"No. Or at least…" Goose bumps were on her arms. "I didn't think he was. But with Steve dead and the guy on the phone telling me that he's going to be coming for me…"

Melinda nodded. "You think Steve might have uncovered his identity."

"I think it's possible."

Mac strode closer to her. "Maybe the killer thinks you know something that can identify him."

Her hands twisted together in her lap. "It's been *eight* years. If I knew something, I would have said it by now." She didn't, though. She didn't know anything about the guy's identity. So she'd just kept moving. Kept going forward. New towns, new people. *A new life.*

"If the killer is in Austin…" Melinda stood up. "You're in danger."

Like she hadn't already figured that out.

"Is that why you stayed silent at the crime scene?" Melinda pushed her with a low question. "Because you were afraid the killer was after you, too?" Before Elizabeth could answer, the detective shook her head. "Staying silent won't save you. It'll just make it easier for you to die."

Well, that was cheery news.

Melinda looked over at Mac. "I guess she has Mc-Guire protection now, huh? I think that's probably a real good thing. Keep me in the loop, and maybe I can do the same for you."

He took out a card and gave it to the detective. Then he escorted the detective outside.

As soon as the door shut behind them, Elizabeth jumped from her seat and started pacing. The sun was up now. A new day. Exhaustion pulled at her, and she really just wanted to go home and crash.

In twenty-four hours, she'd lost the perfect life she'd built. She'd been hunted, she'd found a dead man and now…now all of the dirty little secrets from her past were about to tumble out.

No good. Trouble.

Party girl…always causing trouble.

It's her fault he's dead.

Her palms rubbed against her eyes as she tried to block the flood of memories, but those stupid whispers kept filling her ears.

"Elizabeth?"

He was back. She hadn't even heard the door open. He needed to stop that whole ninja-walking technique he had going on. Elizabeth lowered her hands and turned to face him. "I have to get home."

He nodded. "I'll take you."

No argument? No grilling? No demand to know more about her dead ex?

"You look as if you're about to fall down at any moment." His lips quirked. "Don't get me wrong. You're still as pretty as can be, but I know when a person is about to crash." He lifted his hand toward her, and she found herself reaching out and twining her fingers with his. "You can tell me everything when you wake up."

No, I can't. He had no idea just how tangled her life truly was. Or how hard she'd worked to put the past behind her. She wasn't the same woman. She wouldn't allow herself to be.

The past should have stayed dead. Instead, it had just come killing again.

HE HADN'T COUNTED on the PI.

Elizabeth Snow had aligned herself with a powerful man—or rather, a powerful family. The McGuires were well-known in the area, and frankly, they were trouble that he didn't want.

He watched as Elizabeth and Mac McGuire left McGuire Securities. He kept his phone near his ear, as if he was intently listening to a caller. His hat was pulled down low, and his collar was turned up. He wore sunglasses—not just to hide his face but because his eyes were still red, courtesy of Elizabeth's damned spray.

As the couple headed down the street, he noticed that Mac seemed far more focused on Elizabeth than he was on any potential threats.

That will be a mistake.

But Elizabeth had a way of pulling men to her. Sure, she looked different now. She acted different. And being a librarian? An interesting change for her.

Mac opened his car door for Elizabeth. Then his gaze swept the street.

He turned away before Mac could lock that gaze on him, and he hurried down the street. Now wasn't the time for an attack. It had been easy enough to take out Yeldon. The fool hadn't realized the extent of the danger he courted. And when Yeldon had told him about Elizabeth…

I should have killed her years before. Unfinished business is such a damn pain.

He'd thought Elizabeth didn't know anything that would incriminate him, but now Yeldon had him doubting that truth. He sure couldn't risk any exposure. Too much was at stake. Far, far too much.

Mac's car drove past him.

Elizabeth had talked to a female detective earlier. He'd watched her leave, too. He'd have to find out just what she'd learned…*before* she had time to launch a full investigation that might lead back to him. He'd see if cash would work with her. Often, secrecy and safety were really all about just giving the right amount of money to the right person.

Of course, if the blonde was one of those annoying cops that *couldn't* be bought, then he'd just deal with her in another manner.

So many loose ends… He would be eliminating them all. It was a good thing he was so talented with fixing problems.

Chapter Three

Elizabeth was late for work. Not a little late, but very, very late. She had a 1:00 p.m. shift, but it was close to two when Elizabeth dashed out her front door.

She'd taken five stumbling steps on her sidewalk when she remembered... *I don't have a car!* She'd left it in Austin and—

Her frantic gaze locked on the sturdy frame of her car, parked at the end of her driveway. Relief rushed through her. Mac must have brought it back for her. He'd dropped her off, she'd crashed and had terrible nightmares and now—

Now a man was walking toward her. He'd just exited the SUV parked near Ms. Lee's mailbox. He was tall, with broad shoulders and dark hair. His sunglasses shielded his gaze, but the expression on his face sure looked intent and determined.

Elizabeth staggered and wobbled in her heels. "Stay back!"

"I'm Sullivan."

Sullivan? That name was oddly familiar, and he *looked* familiar, too.

"Mac's brother," he told her as he took off the glasses.

Sure enough, he had the distinct McGuire green gaze. "And I'm your protection for the day."

Her protection? "I thought Mac was handling the case."

"With the McGuires, you don't just get one of us, you get us all."

That was…reassuring?

His hand lifted, and he dangled some keys from his fingertips. "I figured you might need these, considering the way you were racing toward the car."

"Did you bring it over?"

"Mac did."

She took the keys. "Thank you. I—I have to get to work. I called my boss and told her I was running late. I'm *never* late." It seemed important to tell him that. Who knew what he'd already heard about her?

His head inclined. "I'll be tailing you."

He was— "Are you really going to be following me? All day?"

"Just until Mac gets back."

Her fingers curled around the keys. "And where is Mac, exactly?"

"At the morgue."

She backed up a step.

"He's learning more about the dead reporter and seeing if he can discover what evidence the cops have so far."

No, it wasn't all a bad dream. A killer is out there, and he may be watching me. Her gaze darted down the street. Everything looked normal.

"Just how well do you know my brother?" Sullivan asked her as he studied her.

"Not well. I'm his librarian."

Sullivan's dark brows shot up, and his lips curved. "Right."

"I am." She straightened her shoulders. "And like I told you, I'm late. So I really have to hurry." She scrambled past him and unlocked her car. But before she slid in, Elizabeth said, "Thank you. For the protection, I mean. I appreciate it."

He inclined his head toward her. "I get the feeling that if anything happened to you, there'd be hell to pay from Mac. I guess he's pretty fond of his librarian."

What? Shaking her head, she cranked the car and drove away. A quick glance in her mirror showed that Sullivan was coming after her, climbing into that SUV and following right behind her.

Protection.

She shivered.

THE PHONE ON her desk rang hours later and Elizabeth reached out automatically, answering in what she thought of as her professional library voice as she said, "This is Elizabeth Snow. How may I help you?"

"You can die, Elizabeth."

"Excuse me?"

"Should've happened years ago. When you were hiding in that cabin as your boyfriend bled out," his raspy voice said. "The young lovers could've died together."

She shot to her feet. Sullivan was about fifteen feet away, thumbing through a magazine. She waved frantically to him.

"Stop it," that voice snapped. "I can see you." Then laughter. "Do you really think the McGuires are going to stand in my way? I can just eliminate them, too."

She stopped waving. She barely breathed.

"Better, but it's too late. He's already closing in, isn't he?"

Sullivan was marching toward her.

"You'll pay for that," the voice promised her. "You're going to pay for everything."

Click.

"Elizabeth?" Sullivan was in front of her. "What's happening?"

She glanced down at the phone in her hand. "He called me again." Her shoulders hunched as she glanced around the library. Her voice dropped to a whisper as she said, "He's here. He could see me and you."

The staff at the library had already been put on alert about her previous attack, but there were only a few other employees at that location, and the last thing she wanted to do was put any of them in harm's way.

Sullivan's face tensed. "We're leaving."

"I—I can't! My shift still has hours to go—"

"A killer just *threatened* you."

"And you," she told him quietly. "He threatened you, too." She didn't even know who the guy was. A glance at the screen on the phone showed only...*Unknown caller.* Could they trace the call from the library? Surely they could—traces happened all the time on the crime shows she'd seen on TV.

"Come with me," Sullivan ordered. "Now." Then he was hurrying around her desk and taking her elbow. The guy seriously double-timed it as he started rushing her through that library. "Look around," he said, voice curt. "See if you notice anyone who doesn't belong. Someone who sticks out."

They were hunting the killer. Only, she didn't see a

killer. Shouldn't he have stuck out in some way? She saw moms and their kids. She saw the seniors' group. She saw her usual Friday afternoon crowd.

But her stomach was knotted with worry. The guy on the phone *had* been there. He'd seen Sullivan.

Wait, no…he hadn't said that he saw Sullivan.

I can see you.

She stopped walking. "He saw me." There was something about that, something that was bugging her. "He saw me," she said again, and then she was pulling away from Sullivan and hurrying back to her desk. She'd assumed the killer was in the library, but her desk was right next to a big picture window.

A window that looked out to the very busy street.

Her car was parked nearby, just under a sprawling tree. Going on instinct now, she hurried toward the library's exit.

"Elizabeth!" Sullivan called her name and nearly everyone in the library turned to stare. Jeez, didn't the guy know you were supposed to be *quiet* in there?

"He's outside!" She shoved open the door.

He grabbed her and pulled her close. It…it wasn't like when Mac touched her. She didn't get that hot thrill of electricity coursing through her veins. Her breath didn't heave. She didn't—

"What in the hell are you doing, Sully?" Mac demanded, his voice low and lethal.

Her head whipped to the right, and she found Mac standing on the top step leading toward the library. His eyes were narrowed, his face tense, and he sure was giving his brother a furious glare.

"I'm stopping your *librarian* from running into trouble."

Why did he keep saying it like that? Librarians were

awesome. Time for the guy to seriously recognize that fact and stop putting a weird emphasis on the word.

"The killer just called her, and now she's running out to face him. *I* was going to run a trace on the call, but she's dead set to head right into danger."

She jerked away from Sullivan. "He was out here, I know it." Not *in* the library because that wouldn't give him a fast exit. Not with all those people milling around.

She hurried to Mac and caught his hand in hers. "Come on. I think he was on the right side of the building." He would have been able to see her from there.

Mac went with her, but she noticed that he seemed to be shielding her body with every step, moving so that if any threat came, it would have to go through him first. Sweet, protective and—

Her tires were flat. Completely flat. It looked as if someone had just taken a knife and stabbed them.

Sullivan swore.

She turned and looked at the library. Through that gleaming window, she could see her desk. The killer had been right out there when he called her. When he told her that he'd be coming for her and that he would eliminate the McGuires.

I can't let that happen.

"Get that damn trace going, Sullivan," Mac ordered. "Now."

MAC CROSSED HIS arms over his chest and studied Elizabeth. The tension pouring off her filled the room. Her bedroom. She was shoving clothes into her little black suitcase just as fast as she could.

"Running isn't the option you want to take here." He tried to sound reasonable.

She grabbed more clothes, and he saw a sexy scrap

of lace dangling from her fingertips before she pushed the lace into her bag. "You act like this is the first time I've been through a mess like this."

He straightened. "The bozo has come after you before?"

She shook her head. "I don't want you involved anymore. Not you. Not your brother. I'll be fine."

Fine? He stalked toward her and stepped into her path before she could make another clothing run. "Someone wants you dead."

"And *I'll* stop him, okay? I'll deal with this. I'm not running away." Her shoulders straightened. "I'm just going back to the beginning. *That's* the way to end this mess, not running. And not hiding behind the McGuires."

"Protection isn't hiding." And she needed protection. The trace on the call at the library had turned up nothing. No doubt the guy was using a burner phone for his games.

You aren't going to keep playing with her, buddy. Mac wasn't going to let that happen.

"He threatened you. Threatened your family." Her gaze seemed tortured. "You don't know me, Mac. You can't risk yourself—or them—for me." Her voice roughened. "Trust me, you won't think I'm worth that risk."

You're wrong. "You promised me twenty-four hours."

"Because I was exhausted! I wasn't thinking clearly. I should have never involved you." For a moment her brow furrowed. "I still don't even know why you were in that alley."

He stepped closer to her, and her sweet cinnamon scent slid around him. "I followed you."

She backed up. "I—I don't get *why*—"

"I followed you from the library. I waited outside your home, and when you rushed out of that place, I knew something was wrong. I wasn't about to let you ride off alone." Not then, and not now.

"You don't know me," she said again. "Just—"

"I want to know you."

Her lips parted.

"You're sexy and you're smart and every time I go into that damn library, I'm there because I'm looking for you. I'm looking to see if you'll flash that slow smile of yours when I head up to the counter. Looking to see if you'll talk to me just a little bit longer."

"But you— Why?"

He'd just covered the why. "I want you." There, he'd been more than blunt. "I have since the first moment I saw you. And you might think I'm too rough or dangerous for you, but it doesn't change how I feel." *I want you naked in bed with me. I want to be the one to drive you crazy.* Because he would bet his life that she had a fierce wildness chained inside herself. He'd sensed it from the very first moment they'd met.

"You've got danger chasing you now," he said, staying close to her, wishing that she'd open up to him. "And I'm the best man to have at your side right now. I'm not going to flinch away from anything that's coming. You said that jerk threatened my family? That's all the more reason for me to take him down. I don't want him running around loose. He's a killer, and he should be stopped."

He could see the uncertainty in her gaze. "I don't want to drag anyone else into this mess," Elizabeth whispered.

"I'm a PI. I live for this stuff."

She didn't smile. He wanted her to smile. He wanted some of the worry to ease from her beautiful face.

He also didn't want her leaving without him.

"That phone call you got couldn't be traced. This guy is good, Elizabeth. He's covering his tracks and he is hunting you." That infuriated him. "Let me help you. Let me do my job and keep you safe."

"I know," Elizabeth said suddenly, "about your family. I heard what happened to your parents."

Mac didn't let his body tense. Most folks in the area knew about his family. It was hard to keep a double murder hidden. One dark night, while Mac and his brothers had been fighting battles on the other side of the world, their parents had been killed. Their murderers had never been captured. Because of that—hell, *that* was why his family had formed McGuire Securities. To help other victims. To solve crimes that the cops had already marked as "cold" because there was no new evidence in those cases.

"Your family has been through enough. Do you really want me to put them all in more danger?"

"There's one thing about us," he murmured. "We can handle danger."

"Maybe Steve thought he could handle danger, too."

"Maybe," Mac allowed. "But according to the ME, Steve didn't have the chance to put up a fight. He had no defensive wounds at all on his body." Mac had made good use of his time away from her, and he'd been very aware of the ticking clock on that twenty-four-hour period. "The attacker was able to get up close to him, and the guy made one hit—*just one*—a stab right in Steve's heart."

She paled.

"It stands to reason," Mac continued, "that Steve would try to fight off an attacker, *if* he saw the attacker coming."

"He was distracted," she said softly. "Talking to me." Elizabeth cleared her throat. "He might not have even seen the danger..."

Not until the attacker plunged a knife into him.

The sneak attack, the deadly precision...this wasn't some kind of amateur hour. The guy they were after was good—too good.

"And you might not see it, either," she whispered. "The last thing I want is for you to be killed." She stumbled back.

"Do you want to find a knife in your heart, too?" The words were brutal, but they had to be said. "Because when I raced into that alley—" and he would not be forgetting that damn scene anytime soon "—the attacker was there. And he was going for you."

"I managed to fight him off." Her body was stiff.

"He wasn't done, baby." Again, the endearment slipped out. "If I'd been a few minutes later, he could have killed you."

She turned away from him.

"I would have found your body crumpled on the ground, just like his." That infuriated him. And...scared him.

He wasn't supposed to be afraid. Delta Force members didn't show fear. They went straight into battle, and they never backed down.

But when he'd heard her cry out, when he'd stood in that alleyway...

Fear and fury had burned through him.

He went to her and put his hand on her shoulder.

Carefully, he turned her to face him. "I don't want you hurt."

"You shouldn't care about me," she told him. "I'm not who—"

He kissed her. Maybe he shouldn't have. Maybe he should have played the gentleman longer, but he needed to taste her. Needed to see if the passion between them would flare as hot and bright as he'd thought.

It did.

Her mouth opened beneath his. Her hands rose and curled over his shoulders. Elizabeth pressed her body to his, and she kissed him back—not with hesitation, but with hot, fierce need.

Just like that...*just like that*...an explosion seemed to go off inside him. His arms locked around her waist as he pulled her closer. Her breasts pushed against him, her nipples tight, even as his arousal pressed against her. He'd tried to hold back with her, all of those damn trips to the library, books he'd read again and again...

There was no holding back now.

She was trying to leave, trying to walk straight into danger and death, and he couldn't let that happen. Not when he needed her so much.

His tongue thrust into her mouth. She tasted sweet, a light, heady flavor that just made him want more. Her lips slid over his, caressing and tempting, and he wanted to push her back onto that bed. He wanted to strip her. He wanted Elizabeth to stop being afraid and to only think of him.

But...she was pushing against his chest.

He lifted his head. The drumming of his heartbeat pounded in his ears as he stared down at her. "I knew it would be like that," he growled.

"I was afraid it would be," she told him. Her lips were red from his kiss. Her dark eyes gleamed.

Afraid of their desire? Why was that a bad thing?

"I have to stop this guy," Elizabeth said. "I can't be some kind of sitting duck for him."

No, he wouldn't let her be. "You gave me twenty-four hours."

She nodded. Her hands were still on his shoulders. His hands were still enjoying her curves.

"Then stick to your word," he said, trying to keep the desperate edge out of what he was saying. "Give me the rest of my time. You think you'll find out what's happening by going home—back to your past? I say you'll find the truth right here in town. And I'll help you."

Her brows rose. "How?"

"By taking you on a little bit of B and E."

"Breaking and entering?" Her fingers tightened on him. "That's not exactly law-abiding."

No, it wasn't. "Since we'll be breaking into a dead man's home, I don't think he's going to press charges."

Her breath whispered out. "You think we'll find something we can use at Steve's place?"

He nodded. "So what do you say? You going to stick to your word and not run away from me?"

"I just want you safe."

"I will be." *And you will be.* No matter what he had to do, she would be safe.

IT WASN'T HER first B and E. Not really. Long ago, she'd broken into a cabin with her boyfriend. Their car had broken down on a lonely Colorado road. The snow had rolled in, and they'd needed some shelter for the night.

She hadn't known they'd find death out there. She hadn't realized only one of them would ever walk out of that cabin.

"You ready?" Mac asked her.

Elizabeth forced herself to nod. This wasn't some abandoned cabin. This was a house in Austin. They were in the middle of a neighborhood. Totally safe.

Right?

He did something to the lock. She saw the flash of a pick—the guy had come prepared—and there was a faint click. Then Mac was heading inside the house, turning on lights and quickly shutting the door behind them.

It was eerie being in a dead man's home. Everything just looked...frozen. There was a coffee mug near the sink. A folded newspaper was on the kitchen table. A shirt was thrown over the back of the couch.

"You didn't know he was in town?" Mac asked her.

She shook her head. "That's weird, right? That he was here...that I was here..." A coincidence? Or something more?

"I did some checking on him," Mac said as he began to open desk drawers. She noticed that he'd put on gloves. "Apparently, he'd written a few books in the past few years."

She stood in front of Steve's bookshelf. Elizabeth scanned the titles. "*A Knife in the Dark. Murder in the Suburbs.*" Elizabeth glanced back at him. "S.R. Yeldon... I know these titles. They're all true-crime books."

Mac moved to a new drawer. "Right. The guy made his living by taking cold cases and solving them." He exhaled on a long sigh. "Something I admire. Wish I could have met him."

Her heart beat a bit faster. "He must have been work-ing on a story about Nate." That was the only thing that made sense.

"The cops confiscated his computer, so we won't have access to that." He headed into the bedroom and she quickly followed. "But I'm betting he kept some kind of notes. Some backup...*something*."

He opened the closet door. She crept closer to him. He was really confident on this whole break-in thing. "What happens if the cops find us here?"

"We'll get arrested."

Her eyes widened. "You're the one who made me confess all to that detective! And now you—"

He laughed. "Don't worry. I've got an in at the PD I can always use. I was just messing with you."

That wasn't reassuring. She didn't think he'd just been *messing with* her, either.

"What do we have...here?" He reached up and pulled down a brown bag from the top of the closet.

Her brows climbed. "You have a suitcase. That's ex-actly what you have—"

He opened it. Notebooks and photos spilled out.

"Okay, I'm impressed." She knelt on the floor next to the photos. "How did you know that anything was in there?"

"Because all of the other bags were covered in a layer of dust. This one wasn't." He started thumbing through the photos. After a few moments he gave a low whistle. "This is you."

She peered over his shoulder. Yes, that was her. A shot of her that had been taken right after Nate's mur-der. A police officer was pushing her into the back of a patrol car.

For just a moment, a memory of that scene flashed into her mind. So strong and clear.

"Miss...what happened here last night?" The cop's eyes had been kind.

At first, anyway.

"There was so much blood." She leaned forward and picked up another photo. Revulsion poured through her. That shot—it was one of the crime scene photos. Nate's handsome face was so still, and the pool of blood beneath him was clear to see. So much blood.

"In the picture, you didn't have any blood on you," Mac said.

"No...no, I—I only touched him once. To see if he had a pulse." But even then, she'd known it was too late.

Mac's head tilted. "I need to know everything, Elizabeth. Just what went down in your past?"

Hell.

"You know you have to tell me."

"I can't tell you what I don't know." She saw another photo. This one was of the cabin's exterior. The snow had been so white. It had been so cold. She'd been in that closet, shivering, for hours and hours before she'd heard the voices of the police officers.

"Elizabeth—"

"What's in the notebooks?" That mattered. She reached for one, flipped it open, and she saw her name at the top of the page. Her name and age and—

Possible accomplice? The words were written in a rough script.

Her phone rang, making her jump and drop the notebook. She pulled out the phone and read the words on her screen. *Unknown caller.*

"Put it on speaker," Mac instructed her.

She slid her finger over the screen and then hit the icon for the speaker.

"I know where you are," the low voice told her.

"And I'm getting sick of you calling me," Elizabeth fired back.

Mac's gaze shot to her. It seemed like—admiration?—lit his stare.

"Don't worry, Elizabeth. This will be your last call."

A shiver slid down her spine.

"I knew you'd search his house. Did you find the surprise I left for you? *Tick, tick...*"

Mac swore. He grabbed her arm, dragging her to her feet. The photos and the notebooks fell from her lap.

"Stop!" Elizabeth said—the order both to Mac and the psycho on the phone. "I don't know what you—"

"Goodbye, Elizabeth," that voice told her. "You can't hide this time. *I see you.* And the new lover. You'll go out together in a blaze of fury."

A blaze of... Understanding burst through her. He'd said *tick, tick*.

Mac dragged her out of the closet. "There's a bomb! We need to get out of here!"

But the evidence was in there! They couldn't leave the photos and the notebook. She jerked away from him and ran back for the closet.

"Elizabeth, no!" Mac bellowed. Then he grabbed her and—

They didn't make it out.

An explosion shook the house. Fire erupted in a big, tumbling wave, spiraling out from the den. Mac threw his body toward Elizabeth, and they hit hard in the closet, falling even as the world exploded around them.

WHEN THE FIRE lit the sky, he smiled. *Two more problems eliminated.*

That had been easy. He'd made that last call to assure himself that Elizabeth was inside the house. It wouldn't have done for her to be outside when the bomb exploded. But he'd been able to tell by her fear—*you were inside, weren't you, Elizabeth? Did it hurt when the fire erupted? Did you have time to scream?*

The fire was so big and bright. When would a neighbor call the fire department? How long would it be before the victims were hauled out?

The explosion would never be traced back to him. Steve's so-called evidence would be destroyed. The last link—Elizabeth Snow—would be dead.

He didn't have to worry about the past any longer.

Time to concentrate on his future. Retirement was definitely in order.

Chapter Four

Smoke was choking him. The damn fire hadn't killed them—they'd been sheltered from most of the blast, but if they didn't get out of there before the smoke and flames grew too much, they *would* be dead.

"Elizabeth!" He pushed himself up. When the explosion had rocked the house, he'd leaped toward her. He'd pushed her as far back in the closet as he could, and Mac had covered her with his body. "Elizabeth, are you—"

She shoved at him. Hard. "Don't *do* that! Don't leap on me like you're some kind of superhero! Are you crazy? You're not fireproof!"

She was alive. Furious, but alive.

He grabbed a coat and threw it over her head.

"Mac!"

Then he put a coat over his head. He locked his fingers with hers. "We have to get out." He knew that, as soon as they left that closet, they'd be stepping into an inferno. The heat was already nearly singeing him. "Stay low. The coat is to protect you. If it catches on fire—" and it probably would "—then you need to—"

She shoved back the coat and kissed him. Fast. Hard. Not nearly enough for him. "You stay alive, soldier. You understand?" Her eyes seemed to glint with tears. He wasn't sure if those tears were from the fire or from something else.

"Yes, ma'am," he murmured and jerked the coat over her once more. Then he kicked out, not about to touch that doorknob with his hand. Sure enough, flames were everywhere in the bedroom. Eating up the walls. Rolling across the ceiling. He and Elizabeth stayed as low to the floor as they could, but it was apparent really fast that they weren't going to be exiting through the den. That place was already consumed by the fire.

Elizabeth coughed next to him. Flames edged closer.

"Window," he barked out. "Go." It looked as if the glass had exploded outward from the window with the detonation, and smoke billowed out that opening. That would be their escape. They just had to move quickly because he feared the whole house might erupt at any moment. Were there other bombs planted? What about the gas line? That place was a death pit, and they had to get out.

The flames struck out greedily, trying to catch them as they raced past. Chunks of glass were still left in the window, and he punched them out as fast as he could. Then he pretty much threw Elizabeth out the window. He followed her, tumbling out onto the ground.

Elizabeth had tossed away her smoldering coat, and she yanked his away, too. A good thing, considering his coat was now burning. Her fingers caught his and she pulled him up. They ran together, their legs pumping and, sure enough, just when they got to the street, another explosion ripped through the house.

They took shelter behind his car as the house erupted. There was a distinct *boom*, and every car alarm in the neighborhood started shrieking.

Elizabeth didn't look back at the house. She was pressed against Mac, and her hand touched his face. "That was too close," she whispered.

Hell, yes, it had been. Too damn close. And he was very, very glad that she'd decided to make that desperate run back into the closet. If she hadn't, if he hadn't followed her, then they would have been in the den when the first detonation went off—and they would be dead.

He curled his fingers under her chin. His heart was beating far too fast, but his fingers were rock steady. That was the way it always was for him in battle. Fast heart, steady touch. The adrenaline pounded through him and he knew that, later, the crash would rip through his body.

But that was later.

Right then…he kissed her. Not easy. Not soft. He'd come too close to the edge for softness. He kissed with a raw passion and a carnal possession. He wanted her to know exactly how he felt about her—and what he wanted.

What I will have.

She kissed him back the same way, proving that the wildness he'd sensed inside her was really there, just waiting to get out. Waiting for him to set them both free.

Footsteps pounded toward them. He tensed and pulled away from her, rising in a fast crouch—

"Buddy, are you all right?" an older man in a brown robe demanded.

Mac's gaze swept the scene. The neighbors were coming out, rushing to the rescue. That meant the cops and the firefighters would be there soon. Though there wasn't much that they could do.

"We're all right," Mac said as he rose fully. "Thanks."

Elizabeth stood by his side. They turned and faced the house. *Gone.* The fire was still raging, but the house was just a shell now. Any evidence in there would be long gone.

So it's a good thing I managed to save a few items. He could feel the photos and the notebook pushing inside his shirt. He'd shoved them under the fabric moments before they'd fled that fire.

Maybe the killer wanted to get rid of Elizabeth and destroy all of Yeldon's evidence. But the guy had failed, on both counts.

Melinda Chafer glanced at the still-burning wreckage that had been Steve Yeldon's house, then she looked over at Elizabeth. "So once again…you just happened to be at a crime scene?"

This was not going to be easy to explain. "Um, well—"

"We thought the killer might come by and search Yeldon's house," Mac said smoothly. "So we were in the area, keeping watch."

"Keeping watch—is that what we're calling it?" Melinda shook her head.

"You heard the neighbors," Mac replied. "When they found us, we were crouched behind my car, just trying to stay safe from all that flying debris." He whistled. "And just what do you think was inside his house, anyway? Why would someone go to all that trouble to destroy a murder victim's home?"

Melinda pulled out her phone and glanced down at the screen, obviously reading a quick text. Then she focused on them once more. "This could be an accident. A completely unrelated accident. A faulty gas

line. Things like this just happen. Tragic, but that's life."
She narrowed her eyes on Mac. "But what I can't permit is for civilians to get in the middle of an investigation. *My investigation.* Your girlfriend already tried to lie to me once—"

"Uh, I'm not his girlfriend—" Elizabeth began.

Mac frowned at her.

"You're both lucky, damn lucky," Melinda continued, "that you weren't in that house when the fire started. Because then I'd need more body bags." She straightened her shoulders. "I get that the McGuires are a force in this town, but this is *my* case, and I can't have you interfering like this. Don't you see that people are dying?"

Then she turned and hurried away.

Elizabeth waited until the detective was gone, then she asked, "Why didn't you tell her?" He'd been the one who'd been so gung-ho before about being all honest with the cops.

"Tell her?"

"About the photos and the notebook," she whispered. "I know you have them. I saw you in the closet."

Police lights flashed around them. He gave her a slow smile. One that was a little bit scary. "Nice of you to notice," he said.

"Mac?"

"I've got some help on your case," he told her. "At McGuire Securities, we've got a great lady who can work wonders with computers."

Where was this going?

"Funny thing…" Mac murmured. "Our operative discovered that Melinda Chafer deposited ten thousand dollars into her bank account as of nine this morning."

Elizabeth tensed. "And I'm guessing you don't think that was some legitimate deposit?"

"No." His gaze was on Melinda's retreating back. She'd just approached the fire marshal. "I think that payment might have been so she'd overlook a *faulty gas line.*"

He thought the cop was on the take? But—but she liked Melinda. Talk about having bad judgment.

"Until I find out exactly where that money came from and just why it was deposited, I think we'll keep our investigation separate from Detective Chafer's."

She nodded. Elizabeth eased closer to Mac.

If you couldn't trust the cops, then just who could you trust?

His arm curled around her shoulder. "I think it's time we left."

"I WANT YOUR REPORT. First thing, got it?" Melinda kept her focus on the fire marshal. "Before anyone else sees it, you bring it to me."

"Yes, ma'am," he quickly assured her. "But it's going to take some time. A fire this big…hell, it will still be smoldering by dawn."

"But no other houses are in danger? No other people?" Melinda pressed. The last thing she needed was more victims.

He studied the scene. "They should be safe."

Should be. That wasn't nearly good enough for her. "No, they will be. Call in extra personnel if you need them. No one else can get hurt here." Her phone vibrated again, and she pulled it from the clip on her hip. When she saw the screen, she backed away from the fire marshal. She backed away from everyone.

You're welcome.

That text had come through when she'd been talking with Mac and Elizabeth Snow. She'd had no idea what the text meant and now—

Now some bozo had just sent her a text that read.

Pay me back?

Before she could fire off a reply, her phone rang.

Unknown caller appeared on her screen. Frowning, she answered the call and demanded, "Who the hell is this?"

"Did you get my token of appreciation?"

Her jaw locked. She knew exactly what he was talking about—her bank had contacted her earlier. He meant the ten grand that had appeared in her account. "You're setting me up."

"No, I'm appreciating you."

"You've got the wrong woman," Melinda gritted out. "You don't know me, but you can believe I *will* know—"

He laughed. "I know you. I make a point of learning all about my enemies and my allies."

"Oh, yeah? Then which one am I?" *Enemy, you fool. I am—*

"Detective Shayne Townsend... I believe you knew him, rather intimately, correct?"

She stilled at that name. "Shayne is dead." Pain knifed through her at his memory.

"He went out in a blaze of glory, didn't he? Tell me, did you realize that your ex-lover had twisted the law so many times?"

"No." Absolutely not. And that was what she'd told

Internal Affairs again and again when they'd grilled her. *Guilty by association.* But she hadn't been guilty, and she'd known nothing about the secrets that Shayne kept.

"I don't know that I believe you, and if your superiors—or those pencil pushers at IA—were to find out about that ten grand in your account..." He laughed once more. She hated that grating laughter. "What do you think they'd believe?"

Anyone who discovered the money in her account would assume she was on the take. "You—"

"That money can be a token of appreciation or it can be a nail in your coffin, Detective. The choice is yours."

"I can prove I didn't take it!" She was a good cop. She'd worked hard all of these years to earn her place on the force.

"I doubt it," he said, sounding almost bored. "This isn't my first rodeo."

Her gaze flew around. She'd backed across the street. Plenty of people were swarming in the area, but no one was close enough to overhear her conversation.

"Just make sure too much time isn't given into the investigation of Elizabeth Snow's death in that fire," he said.

"What? Elizabeth Snow isn't dead!" Had the bastard meant to *kill* the woman?

Silence.

Melinda knew she'd said the wrong thing. Oh, hell. "Don't you think of it," Melinda ordered. "You stay away from that woman."

He sighed. "You don't sound like you're being a team player, Detective."

"I'm *not* on your team!"

He hung up. She ran back toward the fire, looking desperately for Elizabeth. She'd been there just a few moments before. Where was she?

She wasn't dead?

Rage boiled inside him. Elizabeth Snow had been in the house! She shouldn't have escaped that blaze. He'd watched her go in. He'd called—he'd planned everything!

But she was still on the loose. A wild card that had to be contained. He wasn't sure how many times Steve Yeldon had contacted her before he took out that fool reporter. Elizabeth could know too much. She could remember *too much*.

And that was why she couldn't be allowed to live.

As for the detective…he'd warned her, too. Either she would be his ally or his enemy.

His enemies had an unfortunate habit of winding up dead.

"This isn't my house," Elizabeth said as she leaned forward and peered through the windshield.

Mac's car was a little scraped on one side—courtesy of flying debris from the explosion—but he'd take care of that damage later. Right then his priority had just been getting Elizabeth away from that scene and to safety.

"I know it's not your place," he told her, and he didn't let his lips curl. Odd that, after everything, she actually made him want to smile. "It's mine."

Elizabeth turned to look at him. "Why am I at your house?"

"Because you're spending the night with me."

He easily heard her sharply indrawn breath.

"Look, Mac," Elizabeth said, "that kiss was a heat-of-the-moment thing. Adrenaline and craziness. It wasn't me offering—offering—"

"To jump into bed with me?" Mac asked as he pulled the car into the garage. He'd moved to that home on the edge of the city just a few weeks before. He'd felt closed in, and he'd wanted a new place.

"Right." Her voice was sharp. "I wasn't offering to jump into bed with you."

He killed the engine. "Pity."

"Mac—"

"You're here for your protection." They'd get to the jumping in bed and heat-of-the-moment part again later. "In case you missed it, someone is gunning for you."

"It's rather hard to miss."

Yes, it was. "I've got top-of-the-line security here. Cameras on the outside and inside. No one will get within twenty feet of the place without me knowing about it. You'll be safe here, and after everything that has happened, don't you want a safe place to crash?" *Crash with me, baby. I won't let you down.*

Her shoulders sagged a bit. "Yes."

"Good. Then let's get inside." The garage door had already closed behind them. He hurried around the vehicle and opened her door. "You'll be safe here," he told her once more. "Count on that."

His hand lifted, and he brushed against the soot on her cheek. Would he ever forget seeing her in that room, surrounded by fire? Hell, no, he wouldn't. He hadn't thought they'd get to that window, not in time.

"You can shower, if you want." Because they both smelled like ashes and fire. "You're welcome to use the master bath." He led the way inside, making sure to set his alarm system. He'd installed that system himself, modeling it after the security he and his family had set up at the McGuire ranch.

"You keep doing so much for me." She stopped in his den, looking fragile and lovely and making him want so many things that he shouldn't, not then. "How am I supposed to pay you back?"

"I thought we covered this," he told her gruffly. "We'll deal with payback later."

"Why?" It was a stark question. "Why me? Why did you decide to get involved in my life this way?" She laughed, but it was a ragged sound, not the sweet melody he'd heard before in the library, when she was doing her story times with the kids. "Do you just have some big desire to help lost causes?"

His gaze flickered at that, and Mac moved closer to her. She was about a head shorter than he was, and her body was so much smaller. He'd have to use care with her, always. "You're not a lost cause."

She smiled. "You don't know that for sure. You don't know—"

"You think I don't?"

Surprise flashed on her face.

"You think that I didn't investigate you, right away? Baby, I work for a security company. Our business is discovering secrets. You were tangled up in a murder. Did you think I'd really walk into all of that blind?"

He saw the tremble that shook her.

"I made it my business to know, all right? I pulled up all the police records. I went through all the old news stories. I learned as much as I could about Nate's death…and your involvement."

She took a step back. "And you still want to help me?"

"You were a victim back then. I believe that. You were—"

"I wasn't always a victim. And I sure wasn't always the good girl." She looked away from him. "Do you know how many times I was in juvie back then? Bouncing around, going back and forth. I was pretty much on my own at sixteen, and trouble was something I was very good at finding."

"Until Nate died."

Her lips quivered, then she pressed them together. "Everything changed after that. I became someone new."

"No more finding trouble?"

"No more danger. No more risks. No more walks on the wild side. I couldn't be that person anymore." Her voice seemed hollow. "It was hard enough to just keep going, every single day, knowing that Nate was dead and it was my fault."

Her fault? "It wasn't—"

"I was in the cabin with him. We heard a noise that night, a car coming toward us." Her arms wrapped around her stomach. "We'd broken in to that cabin. Two crazy kids. We thought it was abandoned. That we'd be safe there. We just…" Her gaze fell to the floor. "We didn't have much in the way of families. My mom cut out when I was a kid, and my dad passed away. Nate— he never talked about his family. Never. It was cold that night, and we were just looking for some shelter." A tear trickled down her cheek, cutting through the ash there. "A shelter from the storm."

He waited, hating the pain that he could feel gathering around her.

"We'd made it to Colorado, but we weren't prepared for the snow storm that hit. We broke into that cabin because there wasn't a choice. We thought we'd die if we stayed outside."

But Nate *had* died.

"When we heard the car...the footsteps coming... Nate told me to hide. He said he'd deal with things. I just— I was eighteen. I panicked. I didn't want someone calling the cops on us, so I hid." She swallowed. "But... I think the guy knew Nate. I heard them talking. It wasn't some cabin owner. It was a guy who'd followed Nate out there."

He'd read that account in the police files, but he didn't interrupt. He wanted to hear the full story, from her. It was important—it showed that maybe, just maybe, she was starting to trust him. *I hope the hell so.*

"I was going out there to join them when I heard Nate scream." She rocked a bit, rolling back on her heels. "Nate yelled for me to run and then—then there was an explosion. A gun blast. A blast and then...silence."

He wanted to pull her into his arms.

"I screamed when I heard the gunshot." She confessed this in a whisper. "I screamed for Nate, but he didn't answer, and I could hear footsteps, coming toward me." Her gaze lifted to his. "I knew the shooter was coming to kill me, too."

"But he didn't."

"I ran out the back door. It was so cold out there. So

cold. The snow was coming down, and I didn't have on a coat. I was there, shaking and trying to figure out what to do." She exhaled. "There was firewood near the back door. I could hear him coming behind me. I—I just reacted. I grabbed the wood and I hit him, as hard as I could. The gun blasted again. I guess it went off when he fell. He hit the ground. I—I grabbed the gun and I ran back inside."

He had to touch her. His hand lifted and skimmed down her arm. "You stayed alive."

"I locked the back door. Dragged a chair over and angled it under the door so he couldn't get it open. Then I did the same thing with the front door." Her words were coming faster. "Nate was on the floor. So much blood was around him. He was still and just—dead. I touched his throat, and there wasn't a pulse. The last thing he ever did was warn me to run."

He pulled her against his chest. "He cared about you. He wanted you safe." *I can understand that.*

"I ran back inside because I knew I'd die in the cold. I had to stay in that cabin, but the killer *knew* I was trapped in there. He—he busted one of the windows. I heard the glass shatter. That's when I ran into the closet. I put my back against the wall in there, and I aimed the gun." She was so stiff in his arms. "I was hiding, but if he'd found me, I *would* have shot him."

And she'd stayed in that closet, all night long. Trapped in the cabin with the body of her dead boy-friend. What the hell kind of nightmare must that have been for an eighteen-year-old?

"But I guess..." Elizabeth murmured. "I guess you knew all that, huh?"

He'd known the cold, hard facts. That Elizabeth and her boyfriend had taken shelter in what they thought was an empty cabin. That an unknown assailant had shot Nate. That Elizabeth had been found the next day, still in that closet. Still holding the gun.

She'd been the suspect at first. But there had been no gun powder residue on her fingers. Then they'd found the killer's blood outside, on the wood that Elizabeth had hit him with. They had the killer's DNA, but not him.

For years, he'd eluded police.

"I knew," Mac said softly. But it wasn't the same. Hearing her pain and her fear just gutted him.

She pushed against his chest and he backed away, though he really wanted to just keep right on holding her. "Maybe one day, I'll get you to bare your soul to me," she said.

He'd do it in an instant, for her.

She glanced to the right. "But for now, I think I'll take that shower." She headed for the door, her steps slow.

"Elizabeth!"

She stilled.

"You're not the only one with demons. Trust me on that."

She gave that ragged laugh that tore at him. "My demons won't leave me alone. They're trying to kill me." She looked back at him. "Kill *us.*"

"Not going to happen."

Her lips curved. "There you go, thinking you're some kind of superhero again."

No, not a superhero. Just a man desperate to keep her safe.

A few moments later the bathroom door closed behind her. He headed to his desk. He called Sullivan, keeping an eye on the hallway just in case Elizabeth came back. His brother answered on the second ring. "We've got a big damn problem," Mac told him.

ELIZABETH SNOW WASN'T at home. Melinda Chafer glared at the dark house. Elizabeth and Mac had both vanished from the fire scene, and she'd figured they'd gone to this place.

Guess I figured wrong on that one.

She'd tried calling the number Mac had given her before, but no one had answered there, either. She didn't know if Mac was deliberately avoiding her or if something sinister might have happened.

I need to find them, now. She pulled out her phone. But this time, she called the PD. She'd get Mac's home address and try his place. She'd explain about the tangled mess that was happening with the killer and her bank account and then she'd—

A rustle sounded behind her. Melinda whirled around.

She didn't get to scream. A hard hand slapped over her face, and something sharp jabbed into her neck. She tried to claw out, tried to kick—

But her body already felt weighted down. Far too sluggish.

She was falling—*and someone was catching her.*

"After our little talk," he murmured, "I realized that I just couldn't count on you to be an ally. Pity. You're about to see what happens to my enemies."

She had to get her gun. She had to fight...
"You should've just been a team player."
She couldn't go out like this.
She wouldn't.

Chapter Five

He knows everything.

Mac knew about her run-ins with the law. About her family—a mother who had just wanted to throw her away. He knew she'd looked for trouble, wherever she could find it.

But that stopped with Nate. He cared about me. I cared about him. We were going to change everything. Together.

Then Nate had been taken away. And she'd been left in that cabin with his ghost.

"Elizabeth?"

She jerked when Mac rapped on the door.

"Elizabeth, are you okay?"

She pulled his robe around her body, holding the lapels a bit tighter, and then her left hand reached for the doorknob. When she opened the door, steam from her shower drifted in the air. "Sorry. I didn't mean to stay in the shower so long." And that was such a lie. She'd been hiding from him.

His hair was wet—he must have used another shower—and he was just wearing a pair of low-slung jeans. His muscled chest rippled, and yes, she couldn't help but notice that hard strength. She'd known he was powerful, but seeing him that way...

Keep your control in place.

She already felt far too ragged around the edges. Emotionally exposed and coming off an adrenaline crash. Oh, that did not make a good combination. Pain filled her, and she wanted that pain to stop.

The girl she'd been would have known exactly how to escape from pain.

By doing something wild.

Only she wasn't that girl anymore. She'd decided that girl had died with Nate. Someone new had taken her place. Someone who didn't take risks. Someone who tried to always play things safe.

She'd gotten her GED. She'd gone to college. Worked day and night, scraping by to pay her tuition. She hadn't dated much, and only men who were *safe*. Men who didn't make her feel so out of control. Men who didn't push her for more than she wanted to give.

She saved her adventures for her books. Books were her haven. When the rest of the world made no sense, she turned to them. She'd always done that, even before Nate. Tried to get lost in other worlds because they made the one she actually lived in fade away.

The perfect escape.

Elizabeth cleared her throat. "I thought I heard you talking to someone."

"Just checking in with Sullivan." He backed up so that she could slide past him. Their bodies brushed, and she felt that sharp pull between them. The awareness that was always close when he was near her. "He's going to monitor the arson investigation at Steve Yeldon's place and let us know what's happening."

"So…Sullivan knows everything about my past, too?" Shame burned through her again. She hated to have her past so exposed. A life that she'd wanted to forget. And she had forgotten…

Why had this started again?

"He knows." Soft. Grim.

They were in his bedroom. His bed—a massive beast with a big, sturdy-looking headboard—was just a few feet away. The wild girl she'd been couldn't help but think of Mac in that bed, with her.

The woman who was trying to keep her control… she edged away from the bed. "Sullivan scares me."

"Sully scares a lot of people."

That wasn't exactly reassuring.

"Don't worry," he added, "you don't have anything to fear from him. Sully is on our side."

His robe slid over her legs. She wasn't wearing anything beneath that robe, and she knew he realized it. Her clothes had been covered with ash, and she'd wanted to wash them before wearing the items again.

She just hadn't thought about the whole being-nearly-naked-with-Mac bit. "Most people are scared of you, too," Elizabeth blurted. She knew that was true. She'd gotten a few not-so-subtle warnings from her coworkers after the first time she'd met Mac. "They think you're a dangerous man."

"I am." He shrugged. "But that's good for you. That means I can take care of the creep out there."

"Not if he comes at you with a gun." The way Nate had been killed. "Or with another bomb. It doesn't matter how tough you are then. You can't fight that."

"That's why we have to find the joker before there's another attack."

Yes, they did.

"But right now you should get some sleep. Take the bed," he told her gruffly. "And I'll—"

Oh, no. That wasn't happening. "It's your bed, you take it. I can go sleep on the couch."

He sighed. "I can sleep in here with you. We can both share the bed, or I'll take the couch. You're not sleeping on that lumpy piece of crap."

The bed was big enough to share. Only there was one problem with that plan. "I want you."

She saw his eyes change. Saw the green darken. Saw his nostrils flare. "You shouldn't say things like that."

Well, if he was going to know all of her secrets… "I want you," Elizabeth told him again. "That's why I've been turning down your dinner invitations. Why I didn't want to go out for a drink with you."

He raked a hand through his hair. "You know that doesn't make sense, right? If you want someone, then you—"

"You make me want to let all of my control go and just feel." He'd be an incredible lover; she had no doubt about that. All that hot intensity that was so very Mac… all of that intensity directed at her. Elizabeth swallowed. "I haven't let go of my control in a very long time. I haven't… I haven't let myself care about anyone." Not since Nate.

His eyes narrowed as he slowly stalked closer to her. "That doesn't seem like a good way to live." Then his hand lifted, and his callused fingertips brushed over her cheek. "Not a good way to live at all. That seems empty. Cold." Mac shook his head. "You don't strike me as being cold in any way."

She sure didn't feel cold right then. Elizabeth was burning up—just from his touch. "It hurts too much when you let go," she whispered. "Because when the world falls to pieces around you, there's only pain left."

His hand slid down and curled under her chin. "I won't let the world fall apart."

He was temptation. Big and strong and sexy. Right in front of her. Fear was a shadow in her mind. Death stalked her once again. She'd tried to escape, but the past wouldn't stop.

"I want you," Mac said. His words were deep and dark, and they sank right through her, pushing that shadow of fear back. "I want you to go crazy with me. I want you to forget everything but me." His thumb brushed sensually across her lower lip.

Her breath came a little faster. She found herself leaning toward him, even though she shouldn't. All of her careful rules couldn't go away in one night. She'd played it safe for so long...

Her tongue slid out and licked the edge of his thumb. It was an accident, wasn't it?

His pupils expanded. "Baby, you're playing a dangerous game. Because *my* control can only last so long." His hand slid away from her chin, and he leaned forward. "Don't push too far." His lips closed over hers. And it was just a kiss, so she let go. She wrapped her arms around him and held on tight. She opened her mouth. She kissed him with hunger and need and the passion that was mounting inside her.

One kiss. A kiss before she crashed into bed. A kiss

to help push away the last of her fear. Her control would hold. One kiss.

Her heart drummed faster. Her nails sank into his shoulders.

One kiss.

He lifted her up. Mac held her easily, and her legs curled around his waist.

One kiss.

His tongue slid over her bottom lip then thrust inside her mouth. His hips pushed against her, and she could feel the hot, hard length of his arousal pressing against her.

One. Kiss.

She wanted so much more.

He backed her up, not near the bed, but against the wall. Her back hit and she kept kissing him. Now was the time to break away. Now was the time to stop.

So why was she arching against him? Why was she loving the hard feel of his muscled chest against her? Why was she biting his lower lip and moaning?

"You are driving me insane," Mac gritted out. "You think I didn't see this fire in you? I did…from the very first. And I knew I had to have it. Have you." He kissed a hot path down her neck, and her head tipped back against the wall.

It would feel so good to let go with him. To give in to her desire.

Their desire.

"I've dreamed about you." His voice was even rougher. "Thought about having you in this bedroom, in my bed…"

His head lifted. Their eyes held.

"Tell me to pull back," he ordered, his voice a rough and sexy growl. "Because I can't, if you don't."

Her hands were still wrapped around him. She knew the choice was hers. The moment hers. She could let go. Or she could hold on to her control.

What will happen tomorrow? In the cold light of day? It won't be the same then.

Softly, she said, "Pull back."

He nodded grimly.

Her legs lowered to the floor as she slipped down. His hands flew out and flattened against the wall on either side of her body. "Give me a second." The rough sound of his voice rolled over her.

She didn't speak. Didn't move. Didn't—

"I know you're not ready," he growled, "for what I want from you."

She wasn't sure just what all he did want. And what all she had left to give.

"But you will be," Mac said, his eyes glittering as he looked at her. "We won't be able to keep this contained much longer."

This. Their attraction. The pure incineration they felt when they touched.

"Sooner or later, we'll come together. And it will be damn incredible." He pushed away from the wall. *From me.* "You take the bed. I'll go for another shower." He headed for the door and muttered, "A very cold one this time."

She watched him leave. Her whole body was tense and far too sensitive. Her nipples thrust against the front of his robe. Her skin felt too hot. And a cold shower... it sure seemed like a good idea to her, too.

Did Mac think he was the only one who had fantasies? If so, he was very much mistaken. He'd been starring in her dreams for a while now. Ever since she'd looked up and seen him standing on the other side of that library counter.

MELINDA'S EYES CRACKED OPEN. Her head was pounding, and her mouth was as dry as a desert. She couldn't see anything, just total darkness. But at least she was alive.

That means I have a chance.

Her hands were bound behind her. Thick, rough hemp rope cut into her wrists. Her ankles were tied to the legs of a chair. The perp had sure secured her well.

Where was he? And could she get loose before he came back?

A door opened then, squeaking on its hinges, and light flooded into the room. She squinted against that light and tried to see his face. She hadn't seen him before, not clearly. Not before the guy had jabbed a needle into her.

"Hello, Detective Chafer," he said. He was standing in front of the light, and she still couldn't clearly see his face. Then he stepped forward, shut the door, and darkness filled the space once again.

She didn't like that darkness. In her experience, monsters always hid in the dark. They did their very worst work in the dark. Most of the murders, most of the beatings…they were always under the cover of darkness.

She drew in a deep breath and tried to prepare for whatever was coming. She'd been shot before. She'd been hurt in the line of duty, and she'd survived. She wasn't going to go out without a fight. "Who are you?" Her voice showed no fear. She *wouldn't* show fear.

"My name doesn't matter so much. It's the job that I do...that matters."

The floor creaked beneath his feet, and she knew he was coming closer. "Just what kind of job is it that you have?" A *job*...she didn't like that. It implied he was some sort of hired gun, and that type of criminal was a whole different beast.

"I'm a fixer. I make problems go away." He touched her shoulder. "I'm very good at my job."

She understood then that she was one of his problems. Damn him. "Is that why Yeldon is dead? Someone called you in to eliminate him?"

"He was a problem," he said softly. "The guy never should have been involved. Some people just can't let the past go."

"And the woman, Elizabeth Snow?"

"I didn't think she knew anything. She was never supposed to be a target. But Yeldon...he made me realize that she was just holding on to secrets. My employer became very concerned about that."

So she was talking to the errand boy. The real threat was the employer. Just who the hell was that?

"I've got many interesting skills," he murmured. "I'm good with guns, bombs, knives..."

Melinda did *not* like where this was going.

"I can show you just how good I am." He paused. "You really should have just taken that money as a token of appreciation. You could have looked the other way, and you wouldn't have been involved at all."

"That's not who I am."

"It's who your lover was."

That burned. She hadn't known that her ex had been a dirty cop. But she'd still been painted with the same brush at the PD—guilty by association. That was why her promotion hadn't come through. Why she'd suddenly been given the short end of the stick when it came to the caseloads.

"Things would have been easier for you if you'd just played ball," he said, sighing. "Too bad."

She stiffened her body. Melinda tried to prepare for whatever was going to come. "I was never so good at team sports."

He laughed. "You think you're going to get away, don't you? That something is going to miraculously happen. You're the smart cop. You'll manage to distract me, you'll get out…" He leaned close, and his breath whispered over her cheek. "But that won't happen. You aren't the first cop I've killed. You won't be the last. I told you, I'm a professional. I'm the Fixer."

Fixer.

Right then she was the problem that had to be fixed.

He backed away. "I'm so glad you had your phone on you. That will make things much easier. No need to bother with a burner phone when I can just use yours."

She saw the glow of the screen light up as he called someone.

"By the way," he said. "Feel free to scream during the call. I think it will really help things out…"

He had the speaker on, and she could hear the phone ringing. Once. Twice.

"Hello?" A male voice. Not groggy at all. Strong. Hard. "Detective Chafer?"

Right. Her name would have appeared on the phone's screen, and, with a sinking heart, she realized just who the *Fixer* had called.

"Did you find the man we're after, Detective?" Mac McGuire asked.

The Fixer said, "Oh, yes, she found him... Or rather, I found her."

MAC FROZE IN front of his fireplace. "Who is this?"

"I'm the man you're looking for. The monster in the dark." Grim laughter followed that announcement.

"Do you have Detective Chafer?" Because the jerk had used her phone to make his call. Maybe he thought that move was smart, that by using the victim's phone, it would make it harder to trace him.

You're dead wrong.

Mac pushed a button on his landline phone so that the speaker option would be enabled. He wasn't alone in the room right then. Sullivan had just arrived for a briefing.

"I'm staring right at the detective," the guy on the phone told him.

Mac mouthed, *He's using her phone. Call the cops. Get a trace.*

Sullivan instantly nodded and took out his own phone. He hurried into the kitchen. Mac knew it would take a bit of time for the techs at the PD to triangulate the call on Melinda's cell, so he needed to keep that caller on the line for as long as possible. "Is she alive?" Mac asked.

"For the moment."

"I don't think I believe you."

Silence, then...a woman's scream.

"Happy now?" the guy taunted.

Hell, no. "What do you want?" Mac cast a quick glance toward the hallway. He'd thought that he heard the creak of a door opening. He'd left Elizabeth an hour ago—talk about one of the hardest things he'd ever done—but was she stirring then?

"Well, I'd wanted Elizabeth Snow to die in that explosion, but *that* didn't happen."

No, it sure as hell hadn't.

Sullivan paced back into the room. *On it.* He mouthed the words back to Mac.

"I know you're protecting her," the guy continued. "I know—"

"He's a professional!" Detective Chafer yelled. "Someone hired him, someone— *Ah!*" Her words broke off with a cry of pain.

There was a gasp near Mac. He glanced back to the hallway and saw Elizabeth standing there. She wore one of his shirts—an old T-shirt that fell to the middle of her thighs. Her eyes were wide with horror, and her hands had lifted to cover her mouth.

"She's right," the man on the line said.

Mac shook his head at Elizabeth. He didn't want her to say a word. He didn't want that man to realize that she was there.

"I am a professional. And the job I was hired to do? It's eliminating Elizabeth Snow."

Elizabeth's hands slowly lowered.

"I don't care about you," the fellow said, sounding annoyed. "I don't even care about this detective who is currently bleeding all over the damn place."

Elizabeth crept forward.

"Collateral damage," the killer explained. "That's what you all are. You're just people who happen to be in the wrong place at the wrong time." His sigh came over the line. "There's going to be more damage, if I don't get to finish my job. You really think your family is so safe out on that ranch? I can find a way past any security system. I can find a weakness anywhere. Your brothers…your sister… I can take down anyone."

Mac glanced at Sullivan and saw a darkening rage on his brother's face. It was the same rage burning through Mac.

"But your family isn't my job. Elizabeth Snow is. I just want her."

Over my dead body.

"So give her to me," the guy said. "And we can end this all right now. I'll be fast. I'll put a bullet right between those gorgeous, dark bedroom eyes of hers. One hit, and it's all over."

Rage was nearly choking Mac. "Not going to happen," he snarled. "You won't get near her, understand me?"

Nothing. The guy didn't say a word.

Elizabeth reached out and touched Mac's shoulder.

"She's there, isn't she?" The man on the phone—the man who Mac planned to personally destroy—asked. "Does she look afraid?"

Mac looked at Elizabeth. She looked damn beautiful. And utterly terrified.

"You were afraid that night at the cabin, too, Elizabeth," the killer said, his voice softening a bit. "Didn't expect you to get the drop on me. You weren't even supposed to be there. Just the guy." His rough laughter slid over the phone. "You're the only one who ever got away from me. But really, it's not my fault—"

"Your boss told you to leave her," Mac guessed. *Melinda had said he was a professional. So he would have been following orders. The order had been to kill Nate Daniels. Not Elizabeth Snow. At least, not back then.*

But something had changed, and now Elizabeth was on the guy's hit list.

"Elizabeth…" The killer drew out her name. "Do you really want this detective to die in your place? Do you want me to go after your protector's family? Are you worth the lives of all those people?"

Elizabeth, don't say—

"Will you let the detective go?" Elizabeth asked, her breath hitching. "If I come to you now, will you let her go?" Her gaze held Mac's. "Will you promise to leave the entire McGuire family alone and just *stop*?"

"My orders were for you and Yeldon, no one else. If you stop running from me, we can end things quickly."

The hell they could.

"I should have been able to kill you at the library." Now he sounded annoyed. "You were supposed to be there alone. All of this trouble could have been avoided, *if you'd just been alone.*"

"So sorry," Elizabeth said, a hard edge to her voice and her face tightening with anger, "that I've made it difficult for you to kill me. What a terrible inconvenience that must have been!"

"It won't be difficult much longer. Even a cat runs out of lives eventually."

They'd kept the fellow on the phone awhile. The cops *should* have gotten that trace by now. Even as he had that thought, Mac saw Sullivan glance down at his phone. He seemed to read a quick text, then when he looked up, savage satisfaction was on Sullivan's face.

We've got him.

"Tell me where to meet you," Elizabeth said. "Tell

me, but promise you won't hurt the detective anymore. Just let her go!"

"Meet me at your house, sweet Elizabeth. Meet me now." And he hung up.

She turned away. Mac's hand flew out and his fingers locked around her wrist. "You're not going anyplace."

She yanked against his hold. "I'm not letting her *die*."

Sullivan was grabbing his coat. "The cops just tracked that call. They're on the way to the location they got, and so am I."

"What?" Elizabeth asked, and hope lit her eyes. "You can help her?"

"We can," Mac told her as his hold tightened on her wrist. "But I need you to stay here. I need you to stay safe. We'll go after that guy." Because he was going to be in that takedown. The killer didn't get to just threaten *his* family like that. "We'll make sure he's locked up and that he can't hurt anyone else."

"I want to come, I want—"

Mac shook his head. "You're the one he wants dead. The last thing I am going to do is put you in his path."

Sullivan approached them. "We're all safer if you just stay here, Elizabeth."

She swallowed. "How does that make any of you safe? I don't want you in danger because of me."

Mac's fingers stroked along the inner column of her wrist. "If you go with me, I won't be able to think past the fear."

"Wh-what?"

"I have to know that you're in a secure location. You *are* secure here. My place is damn safe with the security system I installed. By knowing that you're all right, I can make sure that SOB is caught and locked up." She didn't understand just how far beneath his skin she'd gotten. "Just stay."

Elizabeth's gaze searched his, and after a moment she gave a grudging nod. "Please stop him."

"I will." He let her go and nearly ran to his door. "Count on it."

MELINDA GRUNTED BEHIND the hand that was over her mouth. He'd clamped his gloved hand over her lips when she'd tried to yell the truth to Mac, and the freak had nearly suffocated her.

But now the call was over. Now his hand was sliding away.

"That went well," he murmured.

Elizabeth was going to trade places with her. Elizabeth Snow was going to die. How was that *well* in any twisted universe?

He tossed her phone to the floor, and she heard it shatter. Then she felt the edge of his knife.

"I'm sure a PI like McGuire would have been tracing the call," he murmured. "That would be the smart thing to do. It's what I would have done."

Hope burst inside her. If Mac had traced it, then she could survive! Her brothers and sisters in blue would come, and she'd make it out of this nightmare alive. She'd—

He drove the knife into her stomach.

Pain, burning sharp as he twisted the knife.

"Do you think you'll bleed out before help arrives? It's going to be close…" He yanked out the knife. "Just so you know… I actually hope you do survive. Then the real fun will start. Do you think they'll ever believe you weren't on the take?"

Her shirt was soaked with her blood. She could feel it pumping out of her.

"Will some of them always wonder...were we working together? Then I double-crossed you? Will you live...only to be hated?"

She was so cold. And she *hurt*.

"Maybe you should wish for death. It will probably be easier than facing all of those suspicions."

His footsteps shuffled away. The door opened. The bright light hit her in the face.

Where was he going? Where... "Eliz..."

"I know where she is. Don't worry." He looked back at her. She squinted against that light, trying so hard to see the face of the man—the man who'd killed her.

I'm dying. Too much blood.

"Elizabeth is my job, and I always finish any job that I start."

The door shut. She was left with the darkness.

Chapter Six

"Grant," Mac said, talking into the Bluetooth connection in his car even as he drove hell fast. "Man, I need you to get over to my place. Elizabeth is there, and I want a guard on her." He'd called his oldest brother as soon as he could. Mac didn't like the idea of Elizabeth being alone. The security system was good, but he needed better protection for her.

Grant would be that protection. Grant was an ex-army ranger. An all-around force to be reckoned with. He'd get the job done.

And he also lived damn close by. *So he can get his butt over to my house, pronto.*

"Wait...slow down, man!" Grant's voice was gruff. "Elizabeth? She's... Sullivan mentioned her earlier. She's our new client?" The sleepiness was leaving his voice with each word that he spoke. "What's happening? What's going on?"

"She's the new client." His hold tightened on the steering wheel, and when Sullivan pointed left from his position in the passenger seat—giving him directions that the guy was getting from the police—Mac took a hard left. "She's also in danger. I need—"

"If she's in danger, why the hell is she alone?" Now

Grant was angry. "You know we always put the client first at McGuire Securities." Grant had been the one to push for the opening of the business. It was his baby. "This is the woman you've been mooning over the past few weeks, isn't it? The one you kept sneaking away to see—"

"I do *not* have time for this crap," Mac fired back. He hadn't been sneaking anyplace. He'd gone to the damn library. Like that was some kind of federal crime. "The perp kidnapped a detective, and he's threatening to kill her right now. Sully and I are en route with the cops— we're going to stop him before he can hurt anyone else."

Grant whistled. "All of this happened while I was sleeping?"

"Get to my house," Mac ordered him. "I need you there. I have to know that someone is close to her."

"You can count on me," Grant said simply, and yes, that was the way it was for them. They always watched each other's backs. Always.

The call ended, and Mac drove even faster.

"My contact says for us to take a right at the light," Sullivan told him. "We should be there soon, maybe in the next ten or fifteen minutes."

That didn't seem like such a long period of time. Unless… "You heard Detective Chafer scream, too."

"I did." Then, voice careful, Sullivan said, "We still don't know how she's involved, though. I mean, that money in her bank account hasn't been explained. She could be working with him. Or maybe he turned on her or—"

"Or maybe she's an innocent woman who could be dying." A woman that a hired killer was using. "I know you aren't big on trusting anyone, Sully…"

"Only my family," he replied curtly.

"But not everyone is a liar. Not everyone is out to use and destroy." Sullivan had grown hard over the years. And he was keeping secrets. Mac knew it.

Hell, most people thought that Mac was the McGuire brother to watch out for. That he was too intense. That he carried a brutal edge. He'd heard all those stories and plenty more.

Some of those tales were true. He'd seen and done things that would give too many others nightmares. He hadn't led an easy life. *Easy* wasn't exactly in his vocabulary.

Brutal. Hard. High-risk…yeah, that was his world.

He made no apologies.

Neither did Sullivan.

He's more like me than anyone else.

"It's because of her, isn't it?" Mac asked quietly. This was the only time he'd pushed his brother about the woman in Sullivan's past, the woman that no one else in the family knew about but—

I was there. I saw him with her. I saw him after… Sully had been gutted.

"Don't even go there," Sully snapped. "*Don't.* I don't talk about Celia. You know that." His voice thickened. "Just drive the damn car, bro. Focus on the killer out there, and leave my love life the hell alone."

ELIZABETH PACED TOWARD the picture window in Mac's den. The blinds were closed, and she peeked out carefully, gazing into the night. The caller's voice replayed in her head, both scaring her and infuriating her.

A hired killer had taken out Nate? That made no sense to her. Nate had just been a kid—she and he both had been. Two desperate kids who'd connected. Why would someone want him killed?

She turned from the window and paced to the desk in Mac's study. The photos that he had recovered from Steve Yeldon's place were there, along with one of Steve's notebooks. She opened the notebook.

Possible accomplice? It was the notebook she'd been looking at inside Steve's closet. She scrolled through his notes, reading as quickly as she could.

Nate Daniels was targeted.

Hit put on him.

Family connection.

She frowned and reread that line. Family connection? Nate hadn't told her about his family.

She thumbed through the pages of that notebook. Yeldon had written down all kinds of information. Some things that seemed completely irrelevant and then some things...

Nate's mother...died in a car accident.

She swallowed. Well, that would explain why Nate hadn't mentioned his mom. But it seemed odd... Steve had underlined the word *accident.* Had the reporter thought that something more sinister had happened?

No father listed on birth certificate.

She flipped the page in the notebook.

Father? DNA test was a match.

Then there was just...nothing. All of Steve's other information must have been in the other notebooks— notebooks that had burned in that inferno. Or maybe he'd had computer files, but the cops had Yeldon's computer, and she doubted they'd be turning it over to her anytime soon.

She put the notebook down and picked up the photos.

They'd gotten a little charred. Burned a bit around the edges.

She saw herself getting into the back of the patrol car. She saw Nate's body, with all the blood around him. *Yeldon had written about a DNA match. Had Nate's DNA been taken and tested during the autopsy?*

Or had someone known his dad's identity before Nate was killed?

She picked up another photo. This one was Nate's funeral. Her younger self stood there, away from the few others in attendance. They'd buried Nate in that little Colorado town. An anonymous Good Samaritan had donated the money for the burial and the headstone.

It had been a simple service. In that picture, she saw herself and the handful of cops who'd come to the burial. Steve had also been there that day. She didn't remember him taking the picture, but he must have snapped it.

Then…there was another picture from the cemetery. She was gone. The cops were gone. Nate's grave was covered with a bare amount of flowers. She'd put a rose there before she left. And…

There was a man standing near his grave. A man in a long black trench coat. His head was turned toward the grave, and his shoulders were slumped. Behind him, a big, black car waited.

She squinted her eyes as she stared at that photo. She couldn't remember seeing that guy at the funeral. Things had been pretty hazy for her then but—

The doorbell rang. The photo slipped out of her fingers and fluttered to the table.

The doorbell rang again.

It was still the middle of the night. She was wearing Mac's shirt. No one should be there.

Mac wouldn't ring the doorbell, not at his own house.

She crept back into the den. He hadn't told her that anyone was coming by. She eased closer to the door—

And that was when she saw the lock and doorknob turning.

THE PATROL CARS got to the office building before Mac did. When he pulled up, the cruisers had their lights flashing, and uniformed men and women were racing inside the location.

The place was one of the newly constructed sites in the area. Fancy offices, all hooked up and wired, but no businesses were technically in them—not yet. They were show ready, as the Realtors would call them—and the perfect place to stash a hostage.

Sullivan and Mac rushed for the building. Mac saw cops that he knew, guys who waved him past so he could go forward and figure out what was happening.

EMTs burst out of the building. A stretcher was between them, and Melinda Chafer lay cradled on that stretcher. Her face was chalk-white, and there was blood soaking her shirt. When Mac first saw her, he thought she was already dead.

Then her hand moved.

Not yet.

"What did he do to her?" Sullivan demanded.

Mac raced with the EMTs. They were running for the back of the ambulance, and he knew time was of the essence. "Detective Chafer!" he yelled.

The EMTs loaded her into the ambulance. They were working on her, moving so fast, but...

"Mac..." Melinda rasped his name. "He's...he's going after...Snow..."

An EMT shoved Mac back. "She needs to get to the hospital, now."

"Said he—" Melinda seemed to be fighting to force those words out "—was gonna...finish..."

Mac's whole body iced.

"Help her," Melinda whispered.

The ambulance's siren screamed. A few moments later Mac and Sullivan watched as it raced away.

"The building is clear!" a cop yelled.

Clear? Mac searched for a person in charge and saw a police captain whom he knew—Ben Howard. Ben had been the one giving Sullivan the building's location as they raced to the scene. "Ben! Dammit, what is happening here? Where is he?"

Ben jogged toward him. Breath heaving, Ben said, "He stabbed her." His face hardened. "I had my team searching every inch of this place, but that guy is gone."

Ben was a fit veteran of the force. An African American in his early thirties, Ben had once served as an army ranger with Grant. Ben was one of the officers who often helped out McGuire Securities. And they helped him.

"If you hadn't called us," Ben said, "Melinda would be dead." He gave a grim shake of his head. "She may still die. I'm not sure she'll make it to the hospital."

Neither was Mac. Not with all of that blood loss.

Collateral damage. Hell, no, she wasn't.

"I have to know who I'm looking for," Ben said. "I can't put an APB out for a ghost—and that's just what this guy is. He's vanishing and not leaving anyone behind who can tell me what he looks like."

Mac backed away. "I need to get back to Elizabeth."

"The target," Ben said, nodding. "I already sent men to her house. They're looking for this guy. If anyone suspicious shows up there…"

"I don't think he will be showing up there," Mac said as his gut tightened. "He's a professional. A guy who's been killing for years." *And he wanted Elizabeth. Dammit, when he called…he got confirmation of her location. He heard Elizabeth!* His place had good security, but hell, Mac understood that with the right tools, any security system could be breached.

And this guy isn't an amateur.

Mac knew he was dealing with one cold-blooded killer. "He knows where she is." *My house.* His frantic gaze locked on Ben. "Send patrols to my place, now!"

He raced back to his car, Sullivan at his side. Mac yanked out his phone and frantically dialed Grant. *Be there with her. Be there.*

ELIZABETH SWUNG THE lamp at him. When the big, hulking guy snuck inside, she was ready. Unfortunately, so was he. He grabbed the lamp, stopping it about an inch from his face. His eyes—a dark, familiar green—met hers, but Elizabeth was already launching at him with a fast, vicious kick.

She met her target, and he grunted at the impact, but the guy didn't go down.

His eyes. I know those eyes.

"Why my brother thinks you need protecting," the guy muttered as the alarm system beeped, "is beyond me."

Brother. She'd just attacked another McGuire? Hell, now Elizabeth knew why those eyes were familiar. She

stared up at his face. Handsome, strong, determined—
and a definite family resemblance to Mac.

He reset the alarm and only winced a bit when he
walked. "Sorry to scare you, ma'am," he told her, the
Texas accent a bit more pronounced in his voice than
it was in Mac's. "But you weren't answering the door,
and I needed to make sure you were safe. By the way,
I'm Grant." He glanced at the lamp. "Glad we didn't
break that. Mac would be—"

His phone was ringing.

"Excuse me." He pulled out his phone. "Speak of the
devil…" His finger swiped over the screen. "Mac, I'm
staring right at our new client, and I've got to say…your
shirt looks good on her."

His shirt? Elizabeth glanced down. *Crap.* Time to—

"He's coming, Grant," Mac's voice snarled. "He
stabbed Detective Chafer and cut out of here. I know
he's coming for Elizabeth. Secure the house. Keep her
safe. Cops are on the way, but he's got a lead on us.
He's got—"

The lights went out. She expected the alarm to start
shrieking, but it didn't. For an instant there was no
sound at all.

"I think he's here," Grant said softly. "The alarm isn't
working, so the guy must've shut down the system."

How had he done that? The fact that he *had* done
it—chilled her. *He's too good. He just keeps coming.*

"Don't worry," Grant muttered into the phone, "he
won't get her." The phone's screen went black in the
next instant, and she knew he'd ended the call.

Grant grabbed her arm, proving that he could see
way better than she could in the dark. "The doors are
locked," he told her. "And I'm armed. You're safe."

But was Grant? The guy after her had said that he'd take out the McGuires if they were in his way. She couldn't let Mac's family die because of her.

"Help's on the way," he added as he pulled her straight ahead. They didn't trip on any furniture, so yes, the guy must be seeing like a cat. "We just need to stay calm until they arrive."

She was calm, eerily so. They'd gone into the hall-way, away from all the windows. She could hear the sound of her heartbeat filling her ears. It wasn't fast. Just a dull thud. "He used a bomb before," she whispered. "How do we know he isn't planning the same thing right now? While we're hiding in here, he could be out there, setting this whole place to blow. We could get trapped inside." *And burn to death.*

She felt him stiffen beside her. "Well, damn, that's not a good option," he muttered. "Okay, stay here. I'm going to see if I can get a visual on him outside. I'll figure out just what the perp is doing. If we need to make a run for it, we will." Then he pushed a gun into her hand.

"No," Elizabeth began. "You need—"

"I've got a second weapon in my ankle holster. Trust me, I believe in always being prepared."

Her fingers curled around the gun. She hadn't held a gun in years. Not since Nate and that cabin.

"Stay here. When I come back, I'll give a low whistle so you know it's me."

Elizabeth nodded. *So I know it's you and I don't shoot.*

She really didn't have plans to shoot Mac's brother.

His hand squeezed her shoulder. "I won't go far." Then he was sliding away, moving soundlessly in a way that she wished she could mimic. *The same way*

Mac moved. Her fingers curled around that gun. It was oddly heavy in her grasp, and she remembered the hours she'd spent in that little closet, tensing at every sound, wondering if the attacker would come for her at any moment.

Wondering if—

Gunfire blasted. A hard, fast thunder, and Elizabeth sucked in a sharp breath. She wanted to scream out for Grant, but—

He whistled.

She lowered her gun, only aware then that she'd lifted it and aimed at the darkness. "Grant?" Elizabeth whispered.

"He's coming in. That was Mac's back door being blown to hell. *He's in the house.*"

In the darkness. Hunting.

"He's here," Grant said, "and we're stopping him. Our advantage is that he may not know I'm here. I parked my car down the road a bit. I stuck to the shadows when I came to the house. If he thinks it's just you—" his voice was a bare breath of sound "—then he isn't going to be ready for us when we both attack."

Attack. Right. She knew they didn't have a choice. They had to fight. Maybe even kill. If they didn't, they would be dead.

I can't let Mac's brother die.

There were no more blasts from the killer's gunfire. Just an eerie silence that seemed to stretch too far.

Then...

"Elizabeth..." the killer's voice called from the darkness. "This time, I can't let you live."

She shuddered and lifted her gun. *And this time, I won't let you get away.*

HE COULDN'T DRIVE fast enough. Mac's foot slammed the gas pedal into the floorboard, and he raced through a yellow light. He'd been the one to leave Elizabeth; it had been his mistake. He'd thought that the cops would catch the killer.

I was wrong.

"Slow down, man," Sullivan ordered as he gripped the dashboard. "If we get in a wreck, you're not going to be able to help her."

And if he didn't get back to that house, he wouldn't be able to help her, either.

"Grant is there," Sullivan added. "You know the man understands how to take care of a threat. Trust him."

He did trust Grant. But he also didn't know who they were dealing with. A professional killer, yes—but just how much experience did the guy have? Was he ex-military, too? They already knew the guy could wire a bomb, could shoot well, was deranged enough to take a cop hostage…

A guy like that…there is no predicting what he'll do. Lives obviously didn't matter to him. Not at all.

"You heard him," Mac snapped. "He said he'd take out any collateral damage. Grant is in his way. He might just go through our brother in order to get to Elizabeth."

And he couldn't get there soon enough. Mac locked his jaw and tried not to think of that killer shooting his brother—or Elizabeth.

I'm coming, baby. I'm coming.

"ELIZABETH, WHY DO you like to hide from me?" His voice was close, and she knew he was in the den. Soon enough, he'd be heading for the hallway. The guy hadn't turned on any lights, and she wondered just how the hell

he could be navigating so well in there. He and Grant—
what was up with them?

"These games bore me," he added.

Her lips pressed together. *Then stop playing them.*

Grant's hand brushed against her side. She knew he
was trying to reassure her, but she didn't feel particularly reassured. It was so dark, and that guy was creep-
ing ever closer. She was afraid the gunfire would start,
and she knew she was supposed to shoot in order to de-
fend herself. But...

I can't see. What if I hit Grant? What if—

"Do you like the dark, Elizabeth?"

Grant put his mouth to her ear. "I'm going after the
bastard."

No, no, that was *not* a good plan. She tried to grab
him, but he slipped away.

"I like the dark," the killer continued, his voice carrying easily. She reached out, trying to touch Grant, but
he wasn't there. Her hand hit a door—Mac's bedroom
door. She'd been in that room with Mac hours before,
her body alive with passion and need.

But she'd turned away from him. Played it safe.

Now she could be dying.

*I should have held on to him. I should have taken
everything he had to give me.*

Instead of being afraid. Always afraid.

"Can I tell you a secret?" the killer's voice boomed.
"I don't mind the dark...because I can see every single thing."

He could—

Night vision. Oh, crap, wasn't that what soldiers used
on missions? Hunters? He'd killed the lights so they'd
be his blind prey, and all along...

He can see.

"Grant, no!" Elizabeth yelled.

Gunfire thundered once more. She heard a groan. Someone had been hit. But was it Grant or the killer? She stepped forward, and she wasn't calm any longer. Her racing heartbeat shook her entire chest.

She needed Grant to whistle.

He wasn't. "Grant?"

"Grant can't talk right now," the killer said. "But I'm here."

She wondered if the killer was staring straight at her. Was he already at the end of that hallway? No, no, if he was there, he would have shot her already.

You can't just stand there. You're a target.

Her left hand slapped out and hit Mac's bedroom door. She opened that door, rushing inside. There was light there, trickling in faintly from the blinds. This side of Mac's house faced the street, and the lone streetlamp out there was giving her a little illumination. If she could get the killer to come into the room, she could see him. She could shoot him.

"Elizabeth! How many others have to die before you just let me do my job?"

He sounded so angry. What the hell. She was angry, too. "Come and get me!" Elizabeth yelled, wanting him to stay away from Grant. *Grant can't be dead. He can't.* "Come and get me!" This time, her yell was even louder.

And she heard the frantic thud of his footsteps as he raced down the hallway. Only, he didn't get far. There was a loud crash, as if his body had hit the floor. A gunshot blasted, and he screamed in fury.

She rushed back to the bedroom door, squinting against the darkness in the hall.

A whistle filled the space.

"Takes more than that," Grant snarled, "to stop a McGuire."

She kept her fingers around the gun and slid into the hallway.

Chapter Seven

Mac braked in front of his house and saw the flash of police lights behind him. He'd beat the cruisers there; not a good sign. He'd needed them to already be in the house.

He ran toward his home. All of the lights were out. They shouldn't have been out. The house was pitch-black. He grabbed for the doorknob, but it was locked. He didn't even waste time trying to find his key; he just kicked in that door.

"Elizabeth!" Mac roared her name. The house was dark, like a yawning cave, and he slammed his hand on the light switch, but nothing happened.

Then the cops were behind him, shining flashlights into his home. He saw a body slumped near his hallway. A man's body.

Not Grant.

Mac lunged forward just as Grant and Elizabeth emerged from the hallway. The flashlights hit them, and Mac noticed the blood on Grant's shoulder.

He also saw that—

"Drop your weapons!" the uniformed cops yelled as they burst around Mac.

"That's my brother!" Mac shouted back at them.

"He's not the enemy! It's the guy on the floor that's the attacker!"

The guy who could be dead. Or who could still be a threat. Mac wasn't sure yet. He needed to get across that room and get to Elizabeth, but the cops were all in battle mode, and they were in his way.

Grant dropped his weapon. "You need to secure that man," he called out. "He's not dead."

Just as Grant said those words, the guy jumped to his feet. He had a gun out, and he was aiming at Elizabeth.

"No!" Mac shoved the cops out of his way.

Elizabeth had a gun. He hadn't even noticed it before, but she had the gun aimed at the man who was lunging for her.

"No more games," Elizabeth said. She fired.

The bullet slammed into the man, hitting him right in the chest. But he didn't fall. She shot him again—

Still on his feet.

Grant pushed Elizabeth back, because the attacker was preparing to fire his weapon—

The cops were yelling for everyone to freeze, to stand down—

Gunfire. Thundering all around him. And the jerk still was standing.

Mac slammed into the killer, tackling him hard the way he used to do to the opposing team in high school. They crashed to the floor, and something fell off the guy's head. Looked like some kind of goggles—*night vision, tricky SOB.*

The killer tried to bring up his gun, but Mac pounded the fellow's wrist against the floor, and it fell from his fingers. Then Mac drove his fist into the guy's gut.

What the hell? He hadn't made a hard impact, because the man was wearing a heavy vest. A bulletproof vest. The perp had come well prepared.

The killer's cold laughter filled the room.

The gunfire had stopped. The cops had closed in, and one had his weapon aimed at the attacker's head.

"A bulletproof vest won't save you from a bullet between the eyes," Mac snapped at him.

The laughter slowly faded. The flashlights poured onto them. The killer still had a twisted smile on his lips when he said, "I always finish my jobs." The man stared up at him—and the fellow didn't look like a cold-blooded assassin. The guy appeared...normal. Slightly balding, with a weak chin and small eyes. His face was stark white in all of those lights, and his body was slight, almost thin.

Yeah, the guy looked normal all right, and that normalcy had probably helped him over the years. A professional killer who blended right into the background. Deadly SOB.

Mac rose to his feet. Grant and Elizabeth were standing close by, a cop shielding them. "Not this time," Mac told the killer. "This time the only thing you're going to do is rot in jail. You aren't going to hurt anyone else."

The cops rolled the guy over and cuffed him. While one of the uniformed officers patted the perp down, searching for weapons, Mac turned to Elizabeth and Grant. His gaze went to Elizabeth first, and he had to touch her. He wrapped his arms around her and pulled her close, needing to feel her against him. Alive. Safe.

His body shuddered as he held her.

The killer had come so well prepared...night-vision goggles, a bulletproof vest. He'd been determined to eliminate Elizabeth.

Mac's hold tightened on her. "You're safe now."

But…

Was she? Really?

Because the person who'd hired the killer was still out there. The one who'd set this nightmare in motion was hiding somewhere in the shadows.

"Your brother's hurt," Elizabeth whispered.

Mac pulled back and glanced at Grant.

His eldest brother gave him a grim smile. "Barely a flesh wound. Figured out a little too late that the fellow came prepared for the dark. I dove to the side right before he fired."

Sullivan had also closed in on them. "Scarlett is going to give you hell over that," he said, referring to Grant's wife. "You know she doesn't like it when you get hurt."

But Grant just shrugged. "She will, but that's just what I love about her."

Love. Grant talked about love so easily, but once, he'd tried to keep a cold distance between himself and everyone else around him…until Scarlett had punched right through his defenses.

The way Elizabeth is punching through mine.

He hadn't let her go yet. He just didn't want to stop touching her. She was warm and safe in his arms. And he needed to stay with her.

He had been too afraid.

The cops were hauling the killer out of Mac's house. The lights were still out, but the flashlights were shining in every direction. Mac and Sullivan helped Grant outside, making sure that Elizabeth stayed close. When they cleared the house, he saw the chaotic scene outside with mild surprise. He'd been so intent on getting to

Elizabeth that he hadn't realized a full-on cavalry had come to the rescue.

Half a dozen police cars were outside his house, and two ambulances waited close by.

"We've got a man who needs help!" Captain Howard's voice bellowed when he saw Grant. "EMTs!"

And then Ben Howard was in front of Mac and his brothers.

"Quite the scene," Sullivan murmured. "Didn't expect such a large, uh, tactical response."

"That perp took one of our own. He nearly killed her." Howard's voice was low with a lethal fury. "We were taking him down tonight."

While an EMT directed a protesting Grant toward an ambulance, Mac glanced over and saw the killer being loaded into the back of a patrol car.

"This time, it's him," Elizabeth whispered.

Mac frowned.

"He goes in the back of the car," she added, her gaze on the man who'd tried to destroy her. A ghost from her past. "And I get to walk away."

THEY SPOKE TO the cops for hours. Mac watched his house become crime scene central. There were questions, dozens of them—again and again.

They didn't have many answers. It was the man in custody, the hired killer; he'd be the one with the answers.

If the guy talked.

When the police finally released Mac and Elizabeth, when the darkness had faded and light was slipping across the sky, he took her to the one place where he thought they could have some much-needed privacy. And safety.

The McGuire ranch.

His brothers—Davis and Brodie—had been working to remodel the ranch for a while. Those two had always loved that place. After their parents' deaths, Mac hadn't wanted to be anywhere near that spot. Once, he'd been happy there.

But killers had taken that happiness away.

Now, though, things were different. His brothers and his sister had worked so hard to make new memories for all of the McGuires. So when he drove onto the ranch land, he didn't feel the familiar weight of sadness fill him.

But he did feel peace.

"Are you sure it's okay for me to stay here?" Elizabeth asked from the passenger seat. "I can go back home or check into a hotel."

He didn't want to let her go—not yet. Not when they still didn't know who'd ordered the hit on her. She was exhausted, had dark circles under her eyes, and a fine tension shook her body. In the past twenty-four hours, they'd both maybe grabbed an hour or two's worth of sleep. They needed to crash—and crash hard.

Since his place still had crime unit crews collecting evidence...the ranch was their best bet for a haven. "It's more than okay," Mac assured her. "We'll be using the guesthouse. No one is there, so you'll have plenty of privacy."

"I, um, I got your older brother shot. I don't think your family is going to be real happy—"

"*You* didn't get him shot. Some crazy hired killer did that. You were the one firing that gun you held to protect Grant. No one in the family is going to blame you for anything." If someone sent her so much as a cross look, they'd be dealing with him.

She was silent then, and he cast a quick glance her way. Elizabeth was gazing out the window, her expression wistful. "It's really beautiful here. I can't imagine what it must have been like growing up in a place like this."

He looked out the window. The ranch *was* beautiful. There were horses running behind the fence—that would be because Davis's soon-to-be wife, Jamie, was a vet who loved horses. She'd gotten Davis to buy more recently, and they were beauties.

The land rolled gently, and as the drive snaked to the left, he saw the lake. When he'd been a kid, he had gone fishing out there so many times. Often, he'd snuck away with his sister, Ava. He'd always had a special bond with her. Whenever Ava had looked at him, he'd seen love in her eyes.

She and Mom...they always looked at me that way.

But after their mom had been killed, and after some folks in the area had started spreading vicious gossip that maybe—just maybe—Ava had been involved in that killing, things had changed.

All of the McGuires had become harder. And Ava...

It had hurt to look into her eyes for a while. Because he'd felt as if he'd let her down. Let her down and failed their mother.

I should have protected them. I didn't.

"Mac?" Worry had entered Elizabeth's voice.

He turned the car, heading toward the guesthouse. "It is beautiful," he said. He would remember the good times, just as Brodie and Davis had done. He *would* see the good memories that had shaped him.

A few moments later, he braked the car and turned off the ignition.

Elizabeth leaned forward. "That's some guesthouse."

"Davis and Brodie have been on a remodeling kick." That was an understatement. "They expanded the guesthouse. Updated the place."

"It's a house, Mac. There's nothing *guest* about it."

He exited the vehicle and headed around to her side of the car. They'd stopped by her place just long enough to pick up her bag and fresh clothes. Luckily, the bag she'd packed before had been all ready to grab.

When she got out of the car, he couldn't help but admire the way her jeans clung so nicely to her curves.

He might be exhausted, but he wasn't dead.

He had a feeling he'd always be admiring Elizabeth.

She looked up at him. "I know it's not over."

The sun was bright now. He could hear the birds and feel a breeze lightly blowing against him. Everything seemed perfect around them, but the rest of the world was still out there, waiting.

"I know someone hired that man. I know someone put all of this into motion, so I know... I know it's not done."

"We'll deal with it. Whatever is coming, we can handle it." Did she think he was just going to walk away? No, he was in this for the long haul. "But first, you need sleep. Sleep then food, then we'll go from there."

Her lips curled. It seemed as if it had been far too long since he'd seen that slow smile of hers. The one that lit her eyes.

The one that made his heart ache.

"Come inside," he said gruffly. "You're safe here." *With me.*

SHE DIDN'T DREAM of a cold, snowy night. She didn't see the ghost of a boy long dead. She didn't remember what it was like to huddle in a closet, holding a shaking gun in her hands.

Elizabeth slept like the dead. A hard, deep sleep with no dreams. And when she woke, it was to darkness.

The dark scared her, reminding her of what had been and making her tense as she realized—

No, I'm at the guesthouse. I'm safe. Mac is here.

Or he was…somewhere around. She slid from the bed and tiptoed into the hallway, wearing sweats and a T-shirt. When she and Mac had stopped by her house, she'd grabbed the bag that she'd haphazardly packed before, when she'd been planning to run from the danger.

And to go back home.

The guesthouse was quiet. There was no sound except—

A clatter, coming from the kitchen. Her heart lurched in her chest, and she raced down the hallway, worried that someone else had been sent after them and that Mac might be in trouble.

The light was on in the kitchen. And Mac—

Well, he sort of *was* in trouble.

A plate had shattered near his right foot, and a serious mess ravaged the kitchen.

"Mac?"

His head shot up. At first, he looked uncomfortable when he saw her, maybe a bit nervous, and he said, "You're up."

Her brows rose. "You don't sound exactly thrilled about that." What was wrong with him?

He motioned to the madness around him. "I was going to make you a meal, but there wasn't a whole lot to work with here."

He was cooking.

"I can normally cook pretty damn well," he said, and she saw that his cheeks had stained a bit red. "But seriously, Brodie has got to stock this place better. I'm not built for the whole from-scratch baking scene."

She stepped over the broken plate and peered at his creations. Actually, the food looked really good. And her grumbling stomach reminded her that she couldn't even remember her last meal. "You're not going to hear me complain," she said, then she reached out and sampled their "dinner."

"Bread and soup isn't exactly a four-course meal," he muttered. "We can go up to the main house and there will be plenty—"

The bread was melting in her mouth. "Heaven." Amazing. Perfectly moist and sweet, and there was a whole plate of intricate twists that he'd made.

Color her impressed.

He moved their soup over to the table. She kept a hand on the bread. And so yes, she did eat like a desperate woman, but that wasn't something she was going to worry about at that moment. She was just going to eat and thoroughly enjoy herself. When the soup was gone and she'd devoured the last bite of bread, Elizabeth told him, "You are a man with secret skills."

He'd grabbed some wine for them and poured them each a glass. At her words, his gaze seemed to become shuttered, and he took a long gulp of the wine. "Most of my skills…you don't want to hear about."

"Actually, I do." He sat on the other side of the table from her. She had no idea what time it was, and Elizabeth didn't care. What mattered to her right then— Mac. Talking to him. Learning as much about him as she could.

The real world would intrude on them soon enough. The danger and the drama would come calling. For that moment she just wanted to be with him.

"I want to know everything about you," she told him. "Every secret."

He saluted her with his wineglass. "Does that mean I get to learn your secrets, too?"

Elizabeth tucked a lock of hair behind her ear. "I'll answer any question you ask." It seemed like the only fair exchange. She hadn't been close to anyone—not really—for years. In some ways the idea of sharing her secrets was almost a relief.

She'd already pulled Mac into danger. Didn't he deserve to know all about her past?

And she…wanted him to know. It seemed important for him to know all about her life. She was so curious about him. They'd reached some kind of turning point; Elizabeth could feel it. There was no going back for either of them.

"You were Delta Force," she said.

His gaze was shadowed. "First Special Forces Operational Detachment-Delta, yeah, that was me." He poured a little more wine. "I joined the army young, and I always knew I wanted to be Delta."

Since meeting him, she'd read more about Delta

Force and all of the dangerous work that group did. "You worked counterterrorism?"

"Some days. We also engaged in hostage rescue and a lot of direct action assaults." His fingers slid along the stem of the wineglass. "What is it that you want to know, Elizabeth? If I've killed? I have. Did I like it? No, I killed only when there was no choice. When I was fighting to survive or to protect my teammates."

"I already knew that would be your reason."

His eyelids flickered.

"I want to know, why did you become Delta?"

"Because I wanted to make a difference."

That seemed like him. "A true-blue hero."

"Hardly." He drained the wine. "Maybe I'm just an adrenaline junkie. Plenty of folks think so. They say I'm the dangerous one. Of all the McGuires, they think I'm the one you should avoid when the sun goes down and the shadows slip out."

She took another sip of her wine. "Actually, they say that about all of your brothers."

His lips twitched a bit. She liked it when he smiled.

"But you are mentioned as being a bit more…intense," Elizabeth allowed.

His faint smile faded away. "Is that why I scare you? Because I'm intense?"

She needed more wine. "I don't remember saying that you scared me." Quite the opposite. He excited her. He made her want things—so many temptations that she'd tried to resist.

"You know I want you." His voice was a low rumble that rolled over her.

"Yes." And if they were being honest…*say it*. "And you know I want you."

His face hardened. A muscle jerked along his jaw. "You're the one who put the brakes on things before."

Yes, she had been. "I'm not stopping anything now."

Very carefully, he put down his wine. "You should know, my control isn't at its best now. I thought I was going to find you dead. I was desperate to get to you—I was pushed too far."

"So was I." While his voice had roughened, hers had gone soft. "Pushed over the edge because I realized I wasn't really living. I've tried to play it safe. I've tried to do everything right." Tried to be so perfect, all the time. Elizabeth shook her head. "And I could have died. Do you know what I thought about right then? When the lights went out and I heard that guy calling my name?"

His gaze burned as it held hers.

"I thought about you, and I wished—I wished so much that I hadn't stopped you. Hadn't stopped *us*. Because you're what I want. You're—"

He was on his feet. He shot around the table and pulled her into his arms. His mouth crashed down on hers, and they both ignited. No other word for it. The passion burned hot and bright, and she kissed him feverishly. She didn't want any control.

No control. No fear. No worries about the past or the future.

Only that moment mattered. Being with Mac mattered. Holding him tight.

Going over the edge—with him.

She'd thought they'd go to the bedroom.

Instead, he stripped her right there. His hands caught the edge of her jogging pants, and Mac pushed them down. The pants pooled at her feet even as he kept kissing her. Then his hands were on her waist, sliding over the curves of her hips, and his callused fingertips slid under the edge of her cotton panties.

She could feel the bulge of his arousal pressing against her. He wore only a pair of low-slung jeans, and there was no way she could miss his need.

Her hands slid over his back. She wanted to touch all of him and—

He lifted her up and put her on the edge of the table. Her legs were splayed, and Mac stepped between them. He kissed a scorching path down her neck. Her head tipped back as she moaned. He was licking her and lightly using the edge of his teeth, sending tremors of sensation shooting through her. The rough fabric of his jeans made her inner thighs even more sensitive, and her eyes tipped closed as she just *felt*.

Need.

Passion.

"I want to see all of you," he said.

He lifted up her shirt and tossed it aside. Her eyes opened, and she stared at his face. *Intense.* Definitely the word to describe him right then. And all of his hot, feral intensity was on her. One hundred percent. His hand reached out and he caressed her breast, skimming his fingers along the nipple.

"So pretty," Mac muttered. "Got to have a taste." Then his head bent, and his mouth closed around her breast.

Her breath choked out, and her fingers clamped around his shoulders.

"Cinnamon," he whispered. "Love the cinnamon."

Elizabeth had no idea what Mac was talking about, and she didn't care. Her legs curled around him as she urged him closer. He was driving her insane with need. She wanted him to feel the same madness.

Her hands slid down his chest. Over the faint scars that marked him. Scars that showed his strength. She lightly traced the marks and felt him go rock hard beneath her touch.

"Elizabeth…"

She kissed his neck, giving him the same sensual treatment that he'd given to her. She licked, she caressed, she let him feel the faint edge of her teeth, then she slid down.

He moved back, but only just a little. Just enough for her to kiss his chest. To press her lips softly to the marks on his body. For her to have a turn licking his nipples. And then her hands went lower. She unhooked his jeans and slid down the zipper.

He caught her hands. "Baby, you are driving me insane."

Good. That was exactly how she wanted him.

Mac kissed her again. Ever harder. Even hotter. And *his* hands were the ones moving now. Sliding between her legs. Pushing up between the folds of her sex. Caressing her. Stroking her. Making her whole body quiver because she could feel her release building.

Her hand flew out, and she grabbed the table to steady herself. She knocked over a wineglass, but she didn't care.

She only cared about Mac and the way he was making her feel.

His fingers pushed into her and withdrew, a maddening rhythm that had her arching into his touch and needing *more*. "Mac." His name was a demand. They'd waited long enough. She needed him.

."Oh, damn, you are gorgeous." And he stroked her more. His fingers slid over the center of her need. Pressing, sliding, pulling her closer and closer to that release.

His fingers thrust into her and he kissed her.

Her climax hit her while she kissed him. It roared through her body, making every muscle go tight. Her eyes squeezed closed even harder as she savored the pleasure pumping through her.

"Yes," he whispered against her mouth. "Baby, yes, and we're just starting."

He kept caressing her, and her flesh was so sensitive now that she shuddered. Only—he pulled away. He stepped back from her.

Oh, no, that was *not* happening. "Mac." Again, his name was a demand.

Then she saw what he was doing. He ripped open a foil packet, sheathed his arousal then was back to her. He positioned himself between her thighs. This time both of her hands clamped tightly around the edge of the table as she balanced herself. She could tell by the blaze in his eyes that his control was gone. He was just as lost as she was, and Elizabeth loved it.

He drove into her, thrusting deep, and she clamped around him. Their gazes held as the passion spiraled between them. Fast and hot. She was panting. He was holding on to her like he'd never let her go. The pleasure mounted again. Her heartbeat drummed in her ears.

She couldn't look away from his green stare. He was gazing at her as if she were the center of his world. As if nothing else had ever mattered to him.

As if nothing else ever would.

Her legs wrapped around his hips, and she surged up toward him, frantic, so desperate and—

Pleasure. It exploded over her, and she saw the same rapture hit him. His gaze seemed to go blind and he shouted her name. His hold was fierce, too tight, but she didn't care. Right then she was far too gone to care.

They rode out that release together, a hot pleasure that drove away all sane thought.

Nothing was supposed to be that good. Nothing. The pleasure wasn't stopping. It kept rolling through her, and Elizabeth couldn't pull in a deep-enough breath.

"So good," Mac whispered. "Knew it would be like this…first time I saw you."

She hadn't known. She'd never realized anything could be this good.

There were no defenses between them. No masks. No shields. She could swear in that moment, as she looked into his eyes, that she was staring straight into his soul.

Mac leaned forward and kissed her.

The need built once more.

Chapter Eight

"Do you know who the hell that guy is yet?" Sullivan demanded as he paced in police captain Ben Howard's office.

"He hasn't spoken since being taken into custody," Ben said as he sat in his chair, expelling a long sigh. "But we've got his prints. We're running them through the system—"

"I don't think that guy is *in* your system," Sullivan said as he started to pace. "He's a professional, and I don't think he's been caught before."

Ben nodded. "But we caught him *this* time."

Only because the guy had been so determined to kill Elizabeth Snow, at all costs. "He went off the deep end on this one. He could have played it cool…gone after her when there was less heat but…"

"But he didn't," Ben said, his voice hardening. "Maybe the guy has been killing so long that he thought no one could ever stop him. I've seen that crap before. Perps think they're untouchable." He grunted. "The guy is plenty touchable now. He's in lockup, and he's not going anyplace."

It didn't make sense to Sullivan. "Why did he have to eliminate Elizabeth right now? Why not wait a few days? Why get so desperate?" He just didn't understand that. "If the guy is really a professional, he should've had more control. He—"

"Maybe he did have more control," Ben cut in, voice turning thoughtful. "Maybe it's his boss who didn't."

Sullivan stilled as possibilities began to buzz in his mind. "The boss got desperate. He thought the reporter and Elizabeth were about to spill his secrets, so he ordered their deaths. Kill them," Sullivan said, thinking this through, "at all costs."

Ben's head inclined toward him. "That scenario works for me. The guy pulling the strings is the one who told the hit man to act. And I can't help but wonder if that same fellow is the one who told him it was fine to kill a cop along the way, as long as it helped to get his dirty job done."

"How is Detective Chafer? Is she going to be okay?" Sullivan asked quietly.

Ben rubbed his hand over his face. "I don't know. The doctors are working on her, but she's in ICU. She just survived one firestorm down here at the station. IA put her through the ringer, trying to see if she was dirty like Shayne Townsend."

Sullivan didn't let his expression alter. Shayne had once been a friend, a close friend, but ultimately the cop had betrayed the McGuires. "And what do you think about her involvement?"

His hand fell. "I think Melinda Chafer is a good cop, and I won't believe otherwise unless someone can show me concrete proof. Hell, that woman was being wheeled back to surgery, and she was still trying to make sure Elizabeth Snow was okay. *That's* a good cop. She was telling the docs that the guy who took her called himself the Fixer and—"

Sullivan stepped toward him. "Did she say anything else?"

Ben shook his head. "No, just that. Over and over again until the anesthesia kicked in, she was saying the Fixer had taken her."

"And do you know of a hit man who goes by that moniker?"

"I don't, but you can bet I'm checking every connection I've got." Ben hesitated. "You McGuires have some pretty handy connections, too."

They did. Legal and not-so-legal. "I'm on it." And he might turn up a result long before the cops did.

There was one person in particular who might be able to help him, but... Sullivan hadn't spoken to her in years. Not since he'd turned his back and walked away.

The hardest damn thing I've ever done. And the one act that haunted him the most. But he'd had a choice to make back then. His family or—

"I want to talk to that guy," Sullivan said abruptly. He knew that Mac would be wanting an up-close-and-personal talk, too.

"*I'm* going to finish talking to him first," Ben told him. "I get my questions answered and then...maybe we'll see if the McGuire family can get a run at him."

Sullivan lifted a brow. "Playing hardball, are you?"

"You're a civilian. You're not supposed to be in there and—"

"Ben." Sullivan's voice was flat. "Don't play games. You know what I am and what I'm not." He kept his gaze on the other man. Ben had connections to Uncle Sam, too. Connections that not everyone understood.

Some jobs just weren't ever passed along to the rest of the world. "Mac and I are going to want some time with the Fixer."

"I thought it might be personal," Ben murmured, "when I saw the way Mac tore after Elizabeth Snow."

Sullivan knew his brother had lost any objectivity where Elizabeth was concerned. The case was definitely personal for Mac, and that could prove to be a very dangerous thing.

THEY'D MADE IT to the bed. Darkness surrounded them, but Elizabeth didn't mind the dark—not then. Not when she was with Mac.

Her whole body ached, but in a good way. She wasn't afraid of anything. And even her past didn't make her tense.

There was more to the world than blood and death. And there was a whole lot more to living than just careful control.

"Is it time for your secrets?" Mac's voice rumbled in the darkness.

Her hand was on his chest, right over his slowly drumming heartbeat. That steady beat reassured her. "What do you want to know?" Elizabeth asked him.

"You grew up in North Dakota…"

Ah, she was sure he'd already dug up this information, but she told him, "Yes, in a small town called Gibson." Such a small place. Not a lot of money. Not a lot of hope.

"How did you meet Nate?"

She smiled at the memory. "I met him at a bookstore. I was staring through the window, and he came up behind me. At first I thought he was looking at the books

in the display. Then I realized he was looking at me."
Her fingers slid along his warm skin. "With Nate, I felt
like that was the first time someone had actually seen
me. *Me.* I was trouble to the others, a bother, so I just got
by on my own. I stole." She admitted this with no emotion. "I took when I was desperate. And I got caught."
More than a few times. "I didn't like juvie, but when I
was hungry and there wasn't any food nearby, what was
I supposed to do?" It was the painful truth. There had
been *nothing* for her. "Nate was driving through town.
He never meant to stay, he told me that. But we clicked."

His body seemed to have tensed beneath her touch.
"You loved him."

"The way that only an eighteen-year-old girl can."
She laughed at herself, thinking of that girl, of the desperate hope that had filled her. "I wasn't alone with
Nate. He didn't look at me…" *Say it.* "He didn't look at
me as if I were trash. He didn't judge me. He looked at
me—even that first moment—like I was the thing he'd
always been searching for."

Just saying the words sounded silly, but they were
true. When she'd caught Nate's gaze in that glass…

"It sounds like he was a smart boy," Mac's voice
rumbled. "Sometimes you see the one thing you *know*
that you need." There was a tension in his voice that
she didn't fully understand.

Elizabeth cleared her throat and continued, "He
asked me to leave North Dakota. He said there wasn't
anything there for us. We'd only been dating a few
weeks, and I—"

"You what?"

"I didn't even hesitate. I gave up that place in an instant. Back then I lived in the moment. People called

me wild, and I was. I was taking my chance at happiness, and I wasn't going to be the girl everyone pitied any longer. I was going to be different. Nate and I—*we* were going to be different. We made plans. We had dreams…" Her voice trailed away. "Then all of that was gone. I'd given up my home…whatever that was worth…and I was in a strange place. The cops suspected me. The reporters harassed me. I had nothing. No one."

His fingers curled around her chin. He kissed her. A fast, hard kiss. "You have me now."

For how long? She pushed the thought away. "I became stronger after that…determined. I knew I could break. I could shatter and fall away. I could die, just like Nate had, and no one would even notice." That was what had hurt the most. She'd grieved over Nate but…who would have grieved over her? "I decided to change. I worked any job I could. I saved every penny, and I made a life for myself." A life surrounded by the books that had given her solace—books that had always been her escape.

After Nate's death, she wouldn't have survived without them. How many sleepless nights had she spent, curled up with a book? She hadn't been able to bear the nightmares, so she'd slipped into another world. And slowly, so slowly, she'd recovered.

"Why'd you settle in Texas?" Mac asked her.

"I like to travel. I move, every few years. Always looking for something new." *Looking for a place that feels like home.* "But…Nate told me that he'd been born in Texas. So maybe I came here because of that. He'd told me that he loved this area, and when a position opened up, I thought—why not? He was from Dallas,

not Austin, but it still just seemed, I don't know—right."
But that had been before a killer came calling.

"I'm glad you came here."

"Even with the trouble I brought you?"

His arm curled around her. "I'm glad," he said again,
simply.

In the dark, she smiled.

"I was too good…" Mac said slowly. "At what I did."

Her head turned on the pillow, moving automatically
toward his voice.

"I realized that just a few months after basic training.
So did my superiors. It all came easy to me, and I was
pushed up the ranks. Given the harder missions. Missions that were the most dangerous, and I loved them."

She waited.

"I've killed, yes. And when I did, I didn't hesitate."
His voice held no emotion. "What does that say about
me?"

"Mac…"

"When I got word that my parents had been murdered, I was on a black-ops mission. By the time I got
back home, they were already buried. There was nothing of them left for me, and my sister—she wouldn't
even look at me. Ava had been a happy, smiling girl
when I left. One of the best things in my world. When
I came back, she was a stranger. And hell, so was I."

It had been easier for her to confess her past in the
darkness. As he talked, she realized the darkness made
it easier for Mac to confess, too.

"I'd only been back in the US for a few weeks when
the CIA contacted me."

The CIA?

"Me and Sullivan. We were both picked for their Special Activities Division."

"I—I haven't heard of that division."

"SAD exists. Most people just don't talk about it. Sullivan and I were both made offers. They wanted us to work for them. Hell, I wanted to escape the pain. My home was gone, and it looked like the perfect option for me."

She knew where this was going. "You signed up."

"No."

Elizabeth blinked in surprise.

"Ava needed me too much. So did Grant. We were trying to figure out who'd taken our parents. I'd already told Grant he could count on me. What I didn't know…" His breath expelled. "I didn't know that Sullivan had agreed to join, *before* our parents died. He'd already committed, and he didn't tell the rest of us."

She thought of Sullivan. Of the deep shadows in his gaze. A shiver slid over her.

"Two months later I got a call from Sully in the middle of the night. He was in trouble. Off the grid. He had no one to trust, and the mission he was on…it was hard to tell the good guys from the bad."

She wondered where he was going with this story. Why—

"I didn't just kill when I was Delta Force. My brother was in danger, Elizabeth. He needed my help, and I would have done *anything* to bring Sully back home." His voice had deepened. "I had to fight to get him back. By the time I found him, it was almost too late. Men on his own team had betrayed him. He thought that *everyone* had betrayed him. He was being held in a pit, more dead than alive, and I—" Mac drew a ragged breath. "I made sure to get him out. I killed, to get him out."

"You protected your family."

"I killed." Flat. "When it comes to the ones I care about, nothing stops me. No one gets in my way. I do anything necessary."

It sounded as if he was warning her. Did he think she was a threat to his family? Oh, jeez, after what had happened to Grant, how could he think any differently? "I'm so sorry about Grant," Elizabeth said quickly, sitting up and pulling the sheet with her. "I never meant for him—"

"You shot to protect my brother. I'll never forget that," he said. She felt the bed dip as he sat up, too. "But you need to always remember, I'm not some easygoing guy. The stories you've heard about me are true. I'm dangerous, Elizabeth. And when I hunt, when I'm pushed too far, I am a perfect weapon."

He wasn't a weapon. He was a man.

In the darkness, her hand rose. She touched his cheek, feeling the stubble that lined his jaw. "You are more than that."

"Don't be too sure." But his head turned, and he pressed a hot kiss to her palm. "You don't know the measures I'd go to…you don't know what I'd do…" His voice trailed off.

"Mac?"

"You don't know what I'd do…to save you."

ELIZABETH SNOW WASN'T DEAD.

The confirmation hadn't come in. The Fixer had screwed up. Again. He'd been paid far too much money for this sort of mistake.

A kill confirmation had been scheduled for five hours ago. With every single moment that passed, rage built. This should never have happened. The whole mess should have been taken care of years ago. When Nate had been put in the ground, the girl should have been buried, too.

Both eliminated, no more problems.

The years had passed so swiftly. Everything had been moving along just perfectly and then…that damn reporter had started poking around. He'd made connections that he shouldn't have discovered. He'd followed a trail that should have *never* existed.

And he'd learned the truth about Nate.

Elizabeth Snow had been working with the reporter. When Steve Yeldon had first called, he'd mentioned the girl.

Not a girl now. A woman who is out to destroy me.

But that couldn't happen. Too many sacrifices had been made. Too much power was at stake. No, Elizabeth Snow couldn't be allowed to expose what she knew.

And if no one else was around to do the job and eliminate Snow…*then I'll just have to do it myself.*

Elizabeth would never see the threat coming.

"I WANT YOU to come and meet my family." As soon as he said the words, Mac saw Elizabeth stiffen.

Dawn had come, and he'd been awake as the sun rose. He'd watched it lift over the lake, a sight he hadn't seen at the ranch in years. When he'd gone back to the guesthouse, he'd found Elizabeth waiting on the porch for him. Fully dressed, her cheeks rosy and her eyes shining, she'd been a gorgeous sight to see.

Her smile had stretched slowly when she saw him

approach. A warm welcome, a look that said she'd been waiting just for him.

When has anyone else ever looked at me that way?

"Um, your family?" She pushed back her hair. He'd noticed that she did that when she was nervous. The quick tuck of her hair behind her left ear was a dead giveaway. "But…they know what happened to Grant, right? They know I got him shot."

She seemed to be stuck on that. It had only been a flesh wound, and Grant was recovering just fine. "They know everything that went down, Elizabeth, and trust me, no one blames you for anything."

Her expression said she didn't believe him.

"Brodie and Davis—my brothers—are up at the big house. Jamie and Jennifer are both up there, too."

"That's a lot of family."

No, actually, it wasn't. He had plenty more family members to go around. His sister lived on a nearby ranch with Mark Montgomery. Grant's wife, Scarlett, was at the hospital with him. And Sullivan—he was down at the police station, gathering intel.

Sully is always trying to work off a debt that the guy doesn't even owe me. With family, there was no debt.

"I'd like you to meet them," he said, but he wasn't going to pressure her. If she didn't want to deal with his family right then, he understood. The woman had been through hell. She could—

"Now?" Her voice sharpened.

His brow furrowed.

"Is that them coming right now?" She pointed behind him.

Mac spun around. Sure enough, a black pickup truck was turning in the drive that led to the guesthouse.

"That's them," he said grimly. He shouldn't have been surprised that his nosy brothers had decided to come out for a visit *before* he could lure Elizabeth up to the main house. Brodie and Davis—when they were together—could be particularly difficult.

The pickup braked, and Brodie jumped out first.

Davis followed suit, slamming his door and tossing a friendly wave to Mac.

"How can you tell them apart?" Elizabeth whispered.

Davis and Brodie were identical twins. Davis was the older twin, just by a bit, but he never let Brodie forget that fact. He never let *anyone* forget that fact. Mac leaned toward Elizabeth and murmured, "Brodie is the one smiling."

"*That's* a smile?"

Mac laughed. The sound kind of boomed out of him, but Elizabeth was right. Brodie's smile wasn't exactly warm. No one had ever accused the twins of being the life of any party. But then, compared with Mac…they were thought to at least be more easygoing.

"What in the hell is that sound?" Brodie frowned at Mac. "Is that *you*? You damn well don't ever laugh."

So he didn't laugh much. Big deal. Mac shrugged. "I am now."

Appearing thoughtful, Brodie glanced at Elizabeth. "Yes, you are."

Sighing, Davis hurried forward. He held out his hand to Elizabeth. "I swear, my brothers have manners. They just forget them sometimes, ma'am." He gave her a wide grin. "My name's Davis. I'm the older and wiser twin."

"In your dreams," Brodie fired back.

Elizabeth shook Davis's hand. "It's nice to meet you."

Hmm...there weren't many *nice* things about Davis. At least, most people didn't think so.

Brodie elbowed his twin out of the way. Then he flashed Elizabeth a smile. "You're the reason I keep finding thriller books all over Mac's place, even though the tech junkie has a half dozen e-readers."

Mac actually felt his cheeks burn. Brothers could be such a pain. Maybe meeting the family hadn't been his best idea ever. "It's not half a dozen. And I like paperbacks, too," Mac muttered.

"Yeah, and you like the librarian." Brodie backed up a step. "It all makes so much more sense now."

Elizabeth glanced at Mac.

He tried not to glower at his brothers. Did they all know he'd been mooning over her? He'd thought that he actually played things pretty cool.

"If Mac gives you any trouble," Brodie said with a hard nod, "you just come to me. I'll set him straight."

Mac had to snort at that. "The day *you* can set me straight on anything—"

"Dude, you're talking to your elder," Davis tossed out. "Watch yourself."

The twins were pushing him. Mac's eyes narrowed on them. Had he seriously *wanted* to introduce Elizabeth to them? Had he been having a crazy moment or what?

"You know you're safe out here," Brodie suddenly said. "You don't have to worry about anything, Ms. Snow. We've got great security on the ranch. So while you're staying here—"

"I was just staying for the night," Elizabeth blurted. "Not any longer. I—I'll be going home soon."

Brodie and Davis both turned their steely gazes on Mac.

"That so?" Davis asked as he tilted his head and narrowed his eyes. "'Cause Sully told me the guy in custody isn't talking. The fingerprint checks haven't turned up anything on his ID. Cops don't know who he is, and there's no clue as to who hired him."

"And that," Brodie added, his glittering gaze on Mac, "means she's still in danger. You're really going to let her just waltz out of here?"

Mac opened his mouth to reply.

But Elizabeth waved her hand in front of Davis and Brodie. "Hi, there! Over here! Remember me?"

The twins looked at her, frowning.

"There you go," Elizabeth said, her smile stretching. "That's me. The woman who gets to make decisions for herself." Her hand lifted and touched Mac's chest. "Mac is awesome. A fantastic PI and a great guy, but he doesn't decide what I do or what I don't do. I decide that." She squared her shoulders. "And *I've* already decided that I'm not going to be hiding out here. Grant was hurt protecting me. No other McGuire is going to be targeted."

Brodie's brows climbed. "But we're used to being targeted."

"It's kind of our thing," Davis added. He almost sounded disappointed.

Mac sighed.

"Nobody else in your family is going to be hurt," Elizabeth said determinedly. "I needed a place to crash, so I came here. But I'm not hiding. I'm not ever hiding again." Her chin notched up as she focused on Davis. "You said the guy in custody wasn't talking? Well, maybe he'll talk when I'm the one in the room with him. Because I think I deserve some answers, and I'm going to have them."

Davis's gaze seemed to measure her. Then he glanced back at Mac and ordered, "Marry her."

He wanted to kill his brother.

"Now," Davis added, nodding. "Before she has the good sense to get away from you. Seriously, marry this woman."

Mac looked over at Elizabeth and saw the horror on her face. In that instant, he truly wanted to punch Davis.

"It's not like that," Elizabeth blurted. "We're not— It's not like that."

Well, hell.

"We're not serious." Elizabeth looked rather frantically at Mac. "I just hired him. There aren't any ties between us."

The hell there weren't.

"Oh, man, look what you've done," Brodie muttered. "Seriously, I bet Mac wants to beat the hell out of you right now." He shoved Davis back. "The guy lacks tact. He just meant that he liked you," he hurried to explain to Elizabeth. "Pretty much the only person he can talk sanely with is Jamie. Everyone else doesn't get him. He is so lucky he found that woman." His breath heaved out. "Davis and I just came by because we wanted you to know that you could count on us." His voice had softened. "We're up to speed on your case. We know what a nightmare it's been, and if you need us, we're here."

Davis nodded. "Right. Um, we're here."

"Thank you," Elizabeth told them.

She didn't realize what was happening, but Mac did. His brothers were taking her in—the way they would family—extending their protection around her. He might still want to punch them—particularly Davis—but he knew their hearts had been in the right place.

They usually were.

"How's Grant doing?" Elizabeth asked as worry flickered over her face.

Brodie smiled. "He's in fighting form, don't you worry about that. The docs stitched him up, and Scarlett is making sure he takes it easy. If anyone can get Grant to follow a doc's orders, it's her."

"That's good," Elizabeth said. "When that guy came into Mac's house—"

"Grant said you stayed cool," Brodie added. "And that when the time came for you to pull the trigger, you didn't even hesitate."

Her gaze lowered to the hands she'd twisted in front of her. "I didn't realize he was wearing a bulletproof vest." Her voice had gone hollow. "When I fired, I thought I was killing him."

And she still didn't hesitate.

"I had to protect Grant." She glanced over at Mac. "And I wasn't ready to die."

He sure as hell hadn't been ready for her to die. He never would be.

"I want you to take me to the police station," Elizabeth said to Mac. "I need to talk to the man in custody. I have to find out why I've been targeted."

Like he could refuse her anything. Mac nodded.

Her breath expelled in a relieved rush. "I'll get my

bag from inside. That way, you don't have to bring me back later."

Oh, bringing her back was definitely still on the table.

Elizabeth glanced at his brothers. "It was…interesting to meet you. Something I won't be forgetting anytime soon."

Brodie laughed. "I see why he couldn't stay away from that library. You don't take crap from anyone, do you, Ms. Snow?"

"Not anymore," she said firmly.

Then she hurried inside the guesthouse. When the door closed behind her, Mac glowered at his brothers. "You guys don't even understand the meaning of subtle, do you?"

Davis winced. "Sorry. I just think you need to grab that woman—and hold tight." His face sobered. "You were laughing, man. Laughing. Do you know how long it has been since I heard you laugh? You looked at her, and your whole face lit up."

He hadn't realized…

"Maybe she doesn't see it when she looks at you," Brodie cut in. "But it's obvious to us because we know you…you're in deep with her."

In deep. *Drowning.* But she thought… *There aren't any ties between us.* She was wrong, and he'd prove it.

"We know something bad went down with you and Sully years ago," Brodie said, his voice quiet. "You think we couldn't tell the change? It was like a light switched off inside you."

Because he'd lost his parents and they'd come close—far too close—to losing Sully. His brother had nearly died right before his eyes. His world had been full of fury. Hate. He'd had to fight his way back to normalcy.

His brothers had helped him. His sister had been his light.

Then one day, he'd looked up and seen Elizabeth.

Davis's hand curled around Mac's shoulder. "I just want you happy. We've all had enough hell. We deserve more. *You* deserve more."

But the past wasn't buried—not yet. Not for Elizabeth and certainly not for him. "We still don't know who killed our parents or why." There had been so many false leads and suspicions over the years. At some time or another, all of the brothers had feared *they'd* caused their parents' deaths. That the battles they'd fought had followed them home, and their parents had gotten caught in the crossfire.

And Ava had blamed herself. She'd thought that she should have saved her parents. She'd thought that she should have fought harder for them.

But Ava had done all that she could. They all had.

"We know our mother was keeping secrets," Davis said slowly. "Just like my Jamie, she had to start over with a new life."

Davis had fallen hard for the local vet, and then he'd learned the dark truth that Jamie had tried so hard to keep hidden. *Witness Relocation.* Jamie had been given a new identity and shipped far from home. Only that hadn't stopped the madman after her. He'd tracked Jamie to Texas and almost killed her.

And Davis nearly broke apart.

In the aftermath, though, they'd managed to learn a secret that they'd never expected. Their mother's name had appeared in an old Witness Protection Program database. Once upon a time, she'd been someone else, too. And then she'd been sent to Texas.

Then she met Dad. She fell in love. Stayed here. And none of her kids ever knew about her past.

She'd just told them that her parents had died in a car accident long ago. She'd said that she had no siblings.

Now they didn't know what was true anymore.

"Sully called in some of his government contacts," Davis added. "We're supposed to be hearing back any day."

Mac had also called in a contact—one that he hadn't told his brothers about because that particular contact was tied intimately to Sully. She was the one who could give them the best intel, but he knew Sully would never reach out to her.

Sully hadn't wanted Mac to ever mention her name to the others. They didn't know about the pain in Sullivan's past. The guy had sworn him to secrecy.

The family has enough to deal with, Mac. Sully's rough voice drifted through his mind. *Don't add this.*

"We aren't going to stop until we give them justice," Brodie said, his expression determined. "Every day we get a step closer to that goal. We are going to find the people who hurt them. They *will* pay."

That desire for justice had gotten them through dark times. It had given them purpose. But lately, Mac had begun to wonder…what would happen when they caught those killers? When they were rotting in prison, what then?

The door opened behind him. Elizabeth stood there, holding her bag. He bent and took it from her. Their fingers brushed. Their gazes held.

What then?
He'd realized that he wanted more than vengeance. He wanted life. He wanted happiness. He wanted…Elizabeth.

Chapter Nine

"You *don't* have to do this," Mac said, his hand gripping the chair behind Elizabeth. "You don't have to look at that killer again, much less talk to him. The cops can handle—"

"Sullivan said the guy hadn't spoken a word to the cops and that his prints weren't turning up in any system." Elizabeth kept her voice calm, and she schooled her expression. She didn't want Mac realizing just how terrified she was. "The police captain gave us the all-clear for this. There's going to be a guard in the room every moment, and you'll be here."

His jaw hardened. "I don't like this. *I* don't want you near him."

Her gaze slid around the small interrogation room. A one-way mirror lined the wall to the left of her. Captain Howard was in there, watching. Waiting. The DA was in there, too. The man in custody had declined legal representation. Then, according to the captain, he hadn't said another word.

But he *was* coming into that interrogation room. She was going to face him. And she would be figuring out why he was so determined to kill her.

The door creaked opened behind them. Elizabeth's

shoulders tensed as she glanced back. *He* filled the doorway. No longer covered in shadows or hiding in the night, he stood in the harsh light.

He looked…normal. Incredibly, perfectly normal. He was tall, with slightly thin shoulders. The guy appeared to be in his mid-forties. He had faint laugh lines around his eyes and mouth. His eyes were a light blue, small, his chin a little weak, and his hair seemed to be receding on the top.

The man didn't look like a dangerous killer.

He almost appeared to be…anyone. A businessman. A guy you pass on the street. The fellow in line behind you at the grocery store.

There was nothing memorable at all about him, and perhaps that was part of his power. If the guy truly was some kind of hit man, then a nondescript appearance could be his greatest asset.

"Well, isn't this a surprise." He wore an orange prison uniform, and his hands were shackled in front of him. A cop in uniform led him across the room and shoved the prisoner into the chair across from Elizabeth. "I certainly didn't think you'd come for a visit." He smiled at her.

Again…normal. So scarily normal.

Beside her, Mac snapped, "I see you've decided to start talking again…"

The guy straightened a bit and winced. "You know, a bulletproof vest is all well and good, but it still hurts when you get hit." His head turned toward the one-way mirror. "I think my ribs are broken! I need to go to the hospital!"

"You aren't going anyplace," Mac said flatly.

The guy looked back at him. "We'll see about that."

He smirked. "I have a feeling I'll be getting to do pretty much anything I want, real soon."

"Who are you?" Elizabeth asked.

"The Fixer." His smirk stretched. "At least, that's what my clients call me."

He's a hit man. And the guy just admitted it.

"I had lots of time to think in here, and I realized... I have a great deal to offer. For the right price, of course."

She slumped back in her chair. "You think you're going to make a deal."

"I think I'm not spending my life in prison. I think I know plenty of things." He shrugged. "Enough things to get me any deal I want."

No, no, that couldn't happen. Panic built in Elizabeth, but she hurried to tamp it down. If the guy made a deal, he could get out—he could come after her again.

She stared into his blue eyes. There was sharp intelligence there, cunning. And evil. "You killed Nate Daniels."

"Did I?" He lifted his cuffed hands and made a show of scratching his chin. "I don't remember that. But then, if a deal was on the table, I'd remember a whole lot more."

"There isn't going to be a deal," Mac promised him. "The DA already told me—he won't offer you anything. You kidnapped a cop. You nearly killed her. You—"

"Nearly?" the man murmured. "Don't you mean I did?"

Mac stared back at him. He'd been given the go-ahead to reveal some new details as he tried to rattle this SOB's cage. "Detective Melinda Chafer survived. As of an hour ago, she has positively identified you as the man who kidnapped her and assaulted her. She told us that you stabbed her. That you bragged about being *the Fixer* while you held her captive."

Some of the smugness left the fellow's face.

"It's easy enough to connect you to Steve Yeldon's murder," Mac added.

"The hell it is! There's *nothing* tying me to—"

"The DA isn't going to make any deal with a man who attacks cops. And as for the cops in here—" Mac glanced around, smiling a cold grin "—just what kind of treatment will you be getting from them? You're moaning about your ribs, but something tells me you might be seeing a whole lot more damage coming your way. Melinda Chafer is a good cop."

"Is she?" the Fixer taunted.

"McGuire Securities has proof that *you* put that money in her bank account. Our techs managed to track that deposit. Did you truly think you were the only one with computer skills? You wanted her to look as if she was on the take. Now we know the truth."

Elizabeth glared at the killer, taking her cue from Mac. If he could play it cool, then so could she. *Don't think about what it was like to be in the dark, waiting for him to attack. Don't think about it.* "You really believe I don't remember you?" She laughed and was impressed with the mocking sound. "I'll testify. You won't see the light of day again. You *won't* be hurting anyone else."

"Sweetheart…" Fury burned in the Fixer's gaze. "You don't need to be threatening me. You need to be running. Because I might be in here, but the person who sent me after you? That person is out there, and your death is the one thing that person craves. You aren't getting away. You aren't—"

"Who is it?" Elizabeth demanded, her voice low. "Who sent you after me?"

He leaped to his feet. The uniformed officer grabbed his shoulders and held the guy in place. Mac had risen, too, his hands fisted and his body tense.

"You think you knew Nate Daniels?" the prisoner shouted. "You knew nothing. *Nothing.* He wasn't up in that Podunk town by chance, but he got distracted by you—*you're the reason he's dead!*"

Elizabeth jumped to her feet. "No, you are. You killed him. You—"

"You changed his plans. Changed everything for him. Stupid kid." His laughter burned her ears. "Thought he'd found love and that nothing else mattered. He was wrong. So damn wrong. If he'd just kept going, if he hadn't stopped for some piece of tail—"

Mac drove his fist into the guy's jaw. The blow was powerful and it knocked the prisoner back, sending him crashing to the floor.

The guard leaped to act, pulling the killer back to his feet and then holding up a hand toward Mac. "Stop!"

The killer's nose was bleeding. "Jerk…broke it," he snarled. "Get me a doctor! Get me a doctor, now!"

Mac stepped closer to the guy. His arm was up, and he looked if he was ready to pound the other man, guard or no guard.

Elizabeth hurried to Mac's side. "Don't." She caught his fist in her hand. "He isn't worth it."

"Arrest *him*!" the prisoner shouted. "He assaulted me! And get me a doctor!"

The interrogation door burst open. The captain and the DA were there. The DA's face was flushed a dark red. "McGuire, get out of here!"

"Mac?" Elizabeth whispered.

Mac gave a grim nod. But his gaze was still on the prisoner. "You and I aren't done."

Before he could swing again, Elizabeth pulled Mac toward the door.

"Just like the other fool!" the killer yelled after them. "You think she matters. You think she's what's important? Look what happened to Nate! He should have just kept driving! Another hour and I never would've been able to touch him, but he screwed up. He saw that cheap piece—"

Mac turned back around. "You don't understand who I am." He cocked his head and studied the prisoner. "Or just how much I can make you suffer. You think you only need to worry about jail? About being locked behind bars?" Mac smiled at him. "You should have done more research. I'm not some scared kid that you can murder in the middle of the night. I have power and connections that you can't even imagine."

The prisoner swallowed, and his Adam's apple bobbed. "And *you* think I don't have connections? You have no idea who you're dealing with!"

"I'm dealing with the Fixer." And Mac didn't sound impressed. "As far as any connections you have, how do you think your clients are going to feel when they realize you're in jail? Do you think for even a minute that they are going to help you? Or are they going to want to make sure you *never* talk, not to anyone, about the things you've done?"

Fury blazed in the prisoner's eyes.

"I'm betting they'll do whatever it takes to shut you up. You might think you have some kind of leverage—" Mac shook his head "—but you have nothing." Then he turned his back on the guy. "Come on, Elizabeth. We got what we needed."

They had? They still didn't even know the guy's name.

She opened her mouth to speak and then, over Mac's shoulder, she saw the prisoner drive his elbow back into the guard's chest. The uniformed cop grunted and stumbled back, and the killer lunged toward Mac, screaming his rage.

Mac grabbed a nearby chair and spun back to face his attacker. Before the perp could so much as touch him, Mac swung that chair against the guy, slamming it into the other man's chest.

The prisoner went down, hard, and he didn't get back up.

"Now," Mac drawled, "I think he might need that trip to the medic." He dropped the chair.

"MAC." ELIZABETH DRAGGED him into the hallway. "We didn't learn enough! That guy is just going to jerk us around. I needed him to tell us—"

"The key is Nate."

She shook her head. "There isn't anything else to learn about Nate! He's dead. He can't help us."

Mac flexed his fingers. "He can. Actually, *you* can. Before we went into that interrogation, Captain Howard told me that they still have the blood and DNA they recovered from Nate's murder scene. *You* hit the killer, remember? You—"

"I...slammed firewood into him," she whispered.

He nodded. "You got his blood and DNA. They're comparing that with the prisoner's. When it's a match, they'll have him."

Her breath heaved out. He was right. If that DNA matched, they'd have the killer, confession or no confession.

"There's more, Elizabeth. I know there is," Mac continued darkly. "Everything that's happening, it's all about Nate. The only reason you're in danger is because of what happened to him. We have to find out why he was up in North Dakota. What brought him there. We figure that out, and then we're on the right track to discovering who has been pulling the Fixer's strings all of these years."

The door opened behind them. Two cops dragged out the prisoner. He was bleeding and groaning, and he snarled when he saw Mac.

"How can we even trust him?" Elizabeth murmured. "The guy could just be messing with us. He's a killer. A kidnapper and—"

"And he's also a guy who just realized he has *no one* to help him. I was serious in there. When his clients find out that he's been arrested, they'll want to shut him up. There is no way they're going to risk having their secrets exposed, and I'm betting that man knows plenty of secrets."

Captain Ben Howard strode toward them. "That little scene didn't go well," he muttered.

Mac smiled. "I actually thought it did."

The DA stormed out. "You assaulted a prisoner!" He pointed at Mac. "I don't want to see *any* McGuires around that man again, do you understand? I don't care how much clout you think you have! I should get the captain to arrest you right now. I should get—"

Elizabeth tensed. "Just hold on," she began, her voice

sharp. She did not like the way that man was threatening Mac. She didn't like it at all.

"You're welcome," Mac said, tipping his head toward the DA.

The guy's face mottled. "Do you have any idea the damage you just did—"

"The perp was attacking a cop," Ben pointed out, rubbing the bridge of his nose. "It's not like Mac here had a lot of choice. Or would you have *preferred* he let a violent prisoner escape from an interrogation room, under *your* watch?"

The DA's lips thinned.

"The prisoner is going to be scared now," Mac said. "He knows he has plenty to lose. That's going to make him want to talk all the more. The man's silence is at an end." His expression hardened. "Your job is going to be keeping him alive long enough for him to talk."

Ben stiffened. "I have my best officers with him now. Nothing is going to happen to him under my watch."

"You might want to double your officer number," Mac instructed flatly. "Because we're not talking about some petty crimes. We're talking secrets that people have and *will* kill to keep quiet. That man is going to be a target, so your team needs to be ready for the attack. It will come."

Ben held his gaze. "It's never easy with you McGuires, is it?"

"Easy is dull," Mac said, rolling one shoulder. "Wouldn't want that."

Swearing, Ben hurried after the prisoner and his guards.

The DA didn't move. "I shouldn't have authorized

that talk," Jamison White said. "That was a mistake I won't be repeating."

Elizabeth took a breath and made herself ask, "Are you going to offer him a deal?"

The DA's eyelids twitched—a small, but telling movement. "It depends on what he has to say to me."

Her heart slammed into her chest. "He's a murderer! He belongs behind bars!"

"He's a tool I can use," Jamison argued right back. "A domino who can make others fall. You don't understand, Ms. Snow. This case isn't just about you."

"No, it's not." Her hands tightened. "It's also about Detective Chafer. You remember her, right? The woman he kidnapped? That guy is twisted. When he hunted me at Mac's place, he was taunting me. Enjoying my fear. You really think you can *deal* with a man like that?" Elizabeth shook her head. "You can't. You'd be a fool to trust him."

Jamison clenched his jaw. "Then I'm a fool. Because I *will* be learning about that man's past. I will get him to tell me everything that he knows, and if I have to deal to do it, so be it. Other victims and their families deserve closure, too." He jerked his thumb toward the front of the station. "Now, I think your time here is done. If I have any more questions for you, I assume I can find you easily enough."

"You shouldn't assume anything," she snapped, but he was gone. The DA had already stormed down the hallway and left her behind.

Elizabeth glared after him. "I don't think I like that man."

Mac's fingers curled around hers. "We got what we needed. Let's go."

Right. He kept saying that, but she didn't feel as if they'd gotten anything. She'd already known that Nate had been in North Dakota. No big surprise. And—

"Would you slow down?" Elizabeth demanded when they pretty much ran out the front of the police station. "We did *not* learn anything. We didn't—"

He turned toward her. "We learned quite a few important things."

She stared at him.

"Nate is the key. Our focus needs to shift back to him. You said he was born in Texas, right? That was one of the reasons you wanted to come here."

Hesitant now, Elizabeth nodded.

"Then we need to get his birth certificate. If he's still got family in the state, we need to talk with them immediately. We need to figure out just why he went all the way up to North Dakota. What was so damn important up there—"

"Important enough that he was killed for?" But wait, that wasn't exactly what the killer had said. He'd told them that if Nate had just kept going…another hour… if he hadn't stopped for her… *Dear God, is it my fault he's dead?*

Mac's fingers curled around her shoulders. "Whatever you are thinking, baby, *stop.*"

She blinked up at him.

"You wear your emotions so clearly. I can see your pain, and I hate it." He leaned toward her and pressed a quick kiss to her lips. "If I could, I'd make sure you never felt any pain ever again."

When he pulled back, there were so many emotions in his gaze. Emotions she didn't understand, not fully. "Mac?"

He shook his head. "You're not ready for that—not yet."

What was he talking about?

Mac backed up a step. "Let's get Nate's birth certificate. We can get his records and go from there."

Elizabeth nodded. "Okay, let's do this."

He smiled at her. "Have I told you how damn sexy you are?"

Her jaw dropped. That man really needed to work on his timing.

"No?" Mac murmured. "My bad. You're the sexiest thing I've ever seen."

She tucked her hair behind her ear.

His hand lifted, and his fingers tangled with hers. "I can see why Nate forgot everything else when he met you."

"Why I got him killed?"

"No." Anger hummed in his denial. "Why you just mattered more than whatever mission he was on up there."

"I don't understand you." She wished that she did.

His fingers squeezed hers. "You will."

"How is he?" Ben Howard demanded as soon as he entered the small medical area at the PD.

The nurse on duty turned toward him. "Broken nose. Possible concussion." She whistled. "Just what happened in that interrogation?"

A very angry McGuire happened.

"This man needs to be transported to the nearest hospital," she told him flatly. "I can't take care of him here."

Behind Ben, the DA swore. Jamison had just entered the room and obviously caught the nurse's words.

"When I evaluated him last night," the nurse continued, "I told you he should be checked out more thoroughly—"

"You told me the bullets hadn't done any permanent damage."

On the exam table, the prisoner groaned.

"I told you they hadn't *penetrated* because of the vest." Her words were clipped. Her blond hair glinted under the bright light. "But he has severe bruising. His ribs are tender and—"

"Transport him," the DA said flatly.

Ben shot the fellow a stunned look. "Are you serious? You know what a threat this man is!"

"I know that I need him alive. In good working order." Jamison pointed toward the guards. "One guard will accompany him at all times. And I'll go, too. If he wants to talk, I'll be there to listen."

Bad plan. Terrible plan. "You shouldn't make a deal with a devil," Ben told him softly. "Things like that have a way of turning back and biting you."

Jamison shot him a glittering glance. "I know how to do my job. Are *your* hands always clean, Captain?"

Ben's jaw tightened.

"We deal with devils all the time. So don't act all high and mighty as if you've never crossed the line. That man there—"

The guy groaned even louder. His nose was still gushing blood. Hell, Mac had sure pounded him. *Mac's lucky the DA didn't order his arrest right then.* But... Ben suspected the DA was a bit afraid of the McGuires.

Most people in the city were.

"That man there has information that I want." Jamison nodded. "And I will be getting him to talk."

"It's your funeral," Ben muttered.

But Jamison wasn't listening. The DA had already moved closer to the groaning prisoner. "You know who I am, right?" Jamison asked.

The Fixer's gaze rolled toward him.

"I'm taking you to the hospital," Jamison said. "I'm getting you the care you need, and in return, you *will* be sharing your secrets with me."

When the prisoner smiled back at Jamison, a chill slid down Ben's spine.

"HOW ARE YOU going to access his birth certificate?" Elizabeth demanded as she paced Mac's office. "You can't search birth records online. You have to request that info in writing through the Texas Department of State Health Services Vital Statistics Unit."

He glanced up at her, his brows raised.

"What?" She shook her head. "I'm a librarian. I know things, okay? Research is my business, and I've actually helped other people track down their families."

The woman was so damn hot. And smart. But he needed to stay focused right then. "Normally," he allowed, "that is the way things work here." The fully legal way. They weren't going that way. "But, baby," he said as his fingers tapped frantically on the keyboard, "have a little faith in me, would you?"

She turned toward him. Elizabeth put her hand on his shoulder and leaned down close to him. They'd gone to McGuire Securities to get some much-needed privacy—and so that Mac could get to work uncovering the mysteries around Nate Daniels.

"How are you getting access to this material?"

He'd just pulled up a PDF copy of Nate's birth certificate.

"That's not legal," she said as her fingers tightened on him. "That's—"

"Connections," he said simply. "I told you, I know a few people in the government." He scrolled down and saw the name of Nate's mother. "Gloria Daniels." Then he looked at the father listed. "Unknown."

"Why would she—"

"Maybe she didn't want the father to know about Nate." He gave a long sigh. "You can't keep secrets forever." His eyes narrowed on the screen. "We're looking at this the wrong way."

"We are?"

"Yeah, we need to see what was happening in Gloria's life the nine months *before* Nate was born."

She tapped his shoulder.

"Let me," Elizabeth said. "When it comes to research, I really do know how to find info pretty well myself. In *legal* ways."

Right. He shot up and gave the woman her space. Her fingers started moving over that keyboard, typing fast.

"You want the year before, right? Well, Gloria was living in Dallas back then. Let's just see if any old news stories have been archived in the *Dallas Times*…"

Now he was leaning over her.

And he saw the hits that came up on the screen.

"She was working in PR," Elizabeth said, scanning the screen. "Here's a picture of her at a fund-raiser…a big political event from the look of things."

Yes, it was one of those perfect press photos. Everyone was smiling for the camera. Mac noted the men in that photo, specifically, the man with his hand around Gloria Daniels's slender waist.

"Wesley Sutherfield," he said, reading the man's name from the screen.

Elizabeth stiffened. "I know that name."

He did, too. It was familiar, ringing a bell, but…

"Wesley Sutherfield. *Wesley.*" Her brow had furrowed as she glanced up at him. "That used to be the name of a politician in North Dakota."

"You sure about that?" But excitement began to beat in his veins. If Sutherfield had lived in North Dakota, *that* would explain why Nate had been in that state. He'd been going up there to find his long-lost father.

Is that what got you killed?

"Yes, yes, I'm sure. I remember there were campaign posters up everywhere for the guy when Nate and I— when we left. He was running for governor. He won in a landslide victory." She started typing on the computer. This time Mac noted that she was searching for both Gloria Daniels *and* Wesley Sutherfield.

The hits came up, one after the other on the *Dallas Times* site.

In each old picture, Wesley and Gloria were together, and he was always touching her. "Lovers," Mac said flatly. Because it was all too easy to read the other man's body language.

"You think…you think the governor was Nate's father?"

Yeah, he did. "I think we're staring at Nate's missing father." No wonder Gloria had listed him as *unknown.* If word had gotten out that the married man had a child with his lover, Sutherfield's career would have crashed and burned.

"Yeldon's notes said he had DNA proof, right?" Mac asked. "I don't know how he did it, but he made the connection to the governor, and somehow he got DNA proof. A link the guy couldn't deny."

Elizabeth started typing again. Only this time…she was pulling up information on the death of Gloria Daniels.

"Car accident," Elizabeth whispered as she read the other woman's obituary. "Nate was in the backseat. A hit and run when he was just a kid. No wonder he didn't want to talk about his mom." Her fingers went back to typing. She hit a news site and found a grainy old photo of the wreck.

Mac swore. It appeared that someone had crashed directly into the driver's side and… "The other driver left the scene?" he said, reading over her shoulder.

She kept searching. "I don't think they ever found the guy."

Mac would call Ben and see if the captain could contact some of his cop buddies and dig up the old accident report. Gloria had been killed just outside Dallas. He knew that Ben had once worked the Dallas beat, so maybe the man could call in a few favors.

"That's the governor today." When she typed in the governor's name, hundreds of stories appeared. And just like that, Mac knew why the guy's name had rung a bell. There had just started to be some talk about the fellow being a potential vice-presidential candidate.

Wesley Sutherfield.

"He's been married for over thirty-five years," Elizabeth said as she pulled up a new article on the man. "If he is Nate's father, then he was cheating when he got

Gloria pregnant." She glanced back at him. "Scandals and politics don't always go so well together."

Mac glared at the guy's image. Wesley Sutherfield smiled back at him. The guy was polished, his white teeth flashing, his suit perfectly pressed. Every inch the perfect politician.

And the perfect killer?

"I think we need to pay North Dakota a little visit."

THE AMBULANCE DIDN'T have its siren on. The vehicle wasn't hurtling through the traffic. The idiots around him didn't care if he suffered.

That's fine. They'll be suffering soon enough.

"I want to know how many people you've killed." It was the DA talking. Still running his mouth off. A guard—a uniformed cop—was nearby, with his hand hovering close to his holster even as he crouched in the back of the ambulance.

They didn't strap me down well enough. Because he'd done a good job of acting as if he was in agony. A man battling pain wasn't usually perceived as a threat.

That was their first mistake.

An EMT leaned over him. "Your blood pressure's too high. See if you can follow this light." The man shined a light right in his eyes.

He didn't follow the light. He turned his head and looked at the DA. "You gonna keep me out of jail?"

The guy—Jamison—hesitated. "It depends on what you tell me."

Everyone had an angle. "I lost count of 'em all." His lips curled. "All those years, the faces just sort of blend together." That wasn't true. He remembered every single one. The first one…he'd vomited then. He'd woken up for nights afterward, that scream of twisting metal and breaking glass in his head.

He'd been a PI, once. Hired to watch. To report. But then he'd been paid extra, if he could just fix a problem and make it go away.

He'd been so nervous. The opportunity had presented itself, and he'd struck.

I could have sworn that I heard her screaming for help.

But those hadn't been her cries. Those cries had belonged to the kid.

The money had helped to soothe his guilt. And he'd learned—really fast—that there was more money to be earned, as long as he didn't mind getting his hands dirty.

So he'd changed. He'd learned to kill without hesitation.

It *had* gotten easier.

The money had made it easier.

And so what if some of the memories still made him wake up, yelling? Memories couldn't hurt you.

He'd saved all of his cash over the years. He'd been set to retire, for good this time, until the hit had been called in on Yeldon and Elizabeth Snow. He liked to finish his business, so he'd taken the case.

Wish I hadn't. Wish I'd kept myself down in the Keys. Down there nobody looked twice at you. Down there a man could truly disappear.

"You don't remember?" The DA leaned closer. "That's not going to help me."

Lean forward a little bit more. Just a bit.

"I need names." The DA inched toward him. "I need dates, I need locations, I need—"

Got you. He grabbed the DA. *They should've strapped me down better.* He slammed his forehead into the DA's face, and the guy howled. The guard was trying to reach for his weapon, clawing at the holster. *Too slow.*

He grabbed the EMT and yanked the guy in front of him. By the time the guard got his weapon out, he'd hurtled that hapless EMT right at the guard.

The gun exploded.

Did it hit the EMT? Like he cared.

He leaped off the stretcher and grabbed a defibrillator. The dumb DA had risen again, and he slammed it into the side of his head.

Then he lurched toward the back doors. He'd jump out and be home free.

"Freeze!" It was the cop shouting at him. The fool really thought he'd obey orders.

He flipped the guy his middle finger and kicked open the door. The ambulance was going faster than he'd realized, rushing down the road, but he could handle this.

"I said *freeze!*"

He jumped.

The cop fired.

He never even felt it when he hit the pavement, but he did remember...

The victims' screams...because I'm screaming now, too.

Chapter Ten

"I've got our flight taken care of," Mac announced when he walked back into his office later. "Before you know it, we'll be in North Dakota."

Elizabeth glanced up from the computer screen. She was still behind his desk, and her fingers were poised over the keyboard. "I found another article from the *Dallas Times*. Wesley Sutherfield *was* in the area at the time Nate's mother got pregnant. He'd come down here for some kind of public policy convention. There was a photo of him taken…"

He hurried to her side.

"See that woman in the background?" Her finger hovered over the screen. "That's Gloria Daniels." She clicked on another tab, and Gloria's obituary picture appeared. "The governor knew her. There's no denying it." She glanced up at him. "Why would he take out a hit on his own son?"

"Because he didn't want his voters finding out he wasn't the family man he pretended to be. I've seen it before. Power will trump blood any day of the week."

She focused back on the screen. "We're going straight to the governor, aren't we?"

"Hell, yes. I'm not giving him a chance to send someone else after you." They'd be on that plane soon, and he'd get answers.

She rose from the chair. Her body brushed against his. "He's not just going to confess. You know that, right?"

"We have evidence to use against him."

Her eyes widened. "Since when?"

He lifted his brows. "Remember the pictures that Yeldon had?" Pictures they'd *borrowed*. "Remember the shot of the cemetery? That one guy who was there, all alone, after everyone else had left?"

Elizabeth nodded.

"I think that was the governor."

"*Thinking* isn't evidence."

He smiled. "It will be once I have some of the techs at McGuire Securities go over the image. I've already called Sullivan. He picked up the photos from my place and he's bringing them all here. If that *is* the governor, then we know he realized Nate was his son."

"The cops didn't take those pictures when they turned your house into crime scene central?"

"They didn't think those pics had value. And I wasn't about to lose my evidence."

But Elizabeth appeared uncertain. "If we're going to stop him, we need stronger evidence. Not just an old photo. We need a confession—we can't let him just get away with what he's done!"

Mac hesitated. "I think this goes back far longer than you realize."

"Wh-what do you mean?"

He'd been considering this, again and again, and his suspicions had mounted. "That image of Gloria's car. Her side was hit so hard…a fatal accident. But the other driver was able to just run away from a scene like that? I contacted Ben, and he was able to pull strings and get that old accident report faxed over. Witnesses said the other driver was a white male, tall, thin. A real average-looking guy."

She sucked in a sharp gulp of air. "I know someone who fits that description."

"A man who makes killing his life," Mac agreed grimly. "It's possible that Wesley Sutherfield feared Gloria would expose him, even back then, so he took her out."

Her lower lip trembled. "But Nate was in the car. He was just a kid—"

"He was still just a kid when the Fixer was sent after him." Grim words. Brutal. "Eighteen, Elizabeth. And the guy was gunned down."

She looked away from him. "You don't have to tell me that. I'll never be able to forget what happened to him." A tear slid from her eye. "I want to give him justice."

He understood that, probably far better than anyone else. Didn't he want to do the same for his family? To give his parents justice? They deserved that.

So did Nate.

A boy who'd chosen love over everything else.

"Elizabeth, I want you to know—" Mac began but his phone rang, cutting him off. Frowning, he pulled the phone from his pocket. He recognized Ben's number and answered immediately. "Have you learned something new? Is the guy talking—"

"He's not going to talk with anyone, not ever again."

Mac could hear the chatter of voices in the background.

"The man tried to escape. He was jumping out of

the damn ambulance when Officer Porter fired at him. The prisoner was dead within minutes of hitting the ground."

Elizabeth stared at Mac with wide eyes.

"We still don't know who the SOB was," Ben continued gruffly. "And now...now all I can say is that we've got another body for the morgue. Without the guy's identity, we're gonna have a real hard time figuring out who the hell hired him."

"I think I have an idea," Mac told him. He reached out and his fingers slid over Elizabeth's cheek. "She won't be targeted again."

"Mac..." Now the captain sounded worried. "What are you planning?"

"A visit to the past." A little trip down memory lane. But he wouldn't be going alone. He'd take backup with him on that trip. And he *would* get to the truth.

Elizabeth wasn't going to spend the rest of her life being afraid. He wanted her to be happy. He wanted her to have the safe home she'd always wanted.

He'd give her that, no matter what he had to do.

Or who the hell he had to threaten.

SHE HADN'T EXPECTED a private plane. When Mac had told her that the flight had been arranged, she'd figured they'd be flying coach back to North Dakota.

They definitely weren't going coach.

They were at thirty thousand feet, flying straight and easy; the pilot and Sullivan were both up in the cockpit, and Elizabeth felt seriously out of place as she sat in the lush leather seat. They'd been flying for a while. She'd actually lost track of the time, consumed by her own thoughts and fears.

"Elizabeth?"

She yanked her gaze off the window.

"What's wrong?"

What *wasn't* wrong? "You didn't tell me—" she waved her hand "—about this." But she'd seen the ranch. All of the land. McGuire Securities. How had she seriously not realized that the guy was loaded? She'd just... she hadn't thought that much about money. She'd only thought about Mac.

His brows rose. "I told you our flight was waiting."

"You didn't say we had a private plane!"

He sat next to her, his shoulder brushing hers. "Is that why you're upset? Look, there was a case...hell, there have been a lot of cases recently where we realized we needed our own transport. We're not just working in Austin any longer. We hop back and forth across the US now. A while back Sully was on the East Coast and—" his voice lowered "—we needed him back pronto. That made us realize that the plane was an investment that we had to make."

"It's quite an investment." She shifted uncomfortably, completely feeling that she didn't belong in that plane.

Maybe I don't belong with him.

"Stop."

Her gaze darted to his face.

"Our security business has done well, damn well. But I'm not the plane. I'm not the business. I'm not anything else." His fingers curled under her chin. "Don't start changing the way you feel about me because of this. It's just a thing, baby. A tool to make our clients' lives easier."

Changing the way you feel about me... Her heart had

stopped at those words. Did he know? Did he realize just how lost in him she was becoming?

"I'm not used to this," she said as she struggled to find the right words to explain how she felt.

He leaned closer, and Mac put his mouth on hers. It was a quick kiss. Soft. Reassuring. "I'm betting," he whispered against her lips, "that you're also not used to being hunted by a killer. Things haven't exactly been normal lately."

No, they hadn't been. And what would she do when things did return to normal? Would Mac still be in her life, trying to take her out for that drink? Or would their time together end?

He began to pull away. Her hand rose and curled around the back of his neck. "Kiss me again," she said.

He didn't even hesitate. His lips took hers. Not soft. Hot. Hard. His tongue thrust into her mouth, and desire poured through her. Being with Mac had been incredible. She hadn't been prepared for the force of the pleasure that had hit her. She'd been so consumed by him. Elizabeth had almost felt as if she'd lost a part of herself, and she hadn't cared.

She'd just wanted him.

She still wanted him.

When he pulled back a bit, she nipped his lower lip.

"We haven't talked about it," Mac growled. His hands were around her waist.

"It?"

"You. Me. The way you made me go out of my head." Then he lifted her up, pulling her close and putting her on his lap. Her knees pushed down on either side of his legs, brushing against the leather.

"Mac…"

"I like it when you say my name like that. Sounds sexy as hell."

Her hands pushed against his shoulder. "Your brother's up front. I shouldn't be doing this—"

"Sully has serious control issues. He'll be in the cockpit until the plane lands. It's just you and me."

Elizabeth stared into his eyes. "You made me go out of my head, too," she confessed softly.

His face tensed. "Baby, do you have any idea how much I want you right now?"

She could feel his desire pressing against the apex of her legs. "Probably as much as I want you." Wrong time, wrong place, but why couldn't she enjoy him, just for a bit? She was worried about what she'd find in North Dakota. The last thing she wanted was for the past to grab hold of her again.

She'd contacted her director at the library and taken a few more days off from her job. Cathy had been more than understanding. She wanted Elizabeth safe. She was a good friend.

And Mac…

He is a good…everything.

Her fingers tightened on Mac's shoulders.

His head bent and he pressed a long, hot, open-mouthed kiss to her throat. His lips were right over her racing heartbeat.

Her eyes slid closed. "I can't remember wanting anyone the way I want you."

He scored her with his teeth. "You know I won't let you go." His hands slid up her back then moved to curl around her rib cage. Mac's fingers rested just under the curve of her breasts. "I won't be able to do it."

Her lashes lifted. She stared down at him and tried

to read the tangle of emotions in his eyes. "What do you want from me?" Maybe she should have asked that question before.

"Everything that you can give me."

Instinctively, Elizabeth shook her head. She didn't even know what she had. *Control.* Control was what she'd known for so many years. Control was key, it was—

He took her mouth again. The kiss was demanding, and she reveled in it.

"Everything," Mac muttered. "Because that's what I'll give you."

This was the first time they'd talked about any kind of future. She usually only focused on the present and tried to bury her past.

Her tongue slid over his lower lip and then thrust inside his mouth. She tasted and she savored and she caressed. The desire built within her, tightening her muscles, making her breasts and her sex so sensitive. He arched up against her, pushing his hips into her. His jeans were between them. Hers were in the way.

They couldn't have sex. Not there. Not with the pilot and Sullivan up at the front of the plane.

They couldn't.

But she wanted to. She wanted to strip him and let go. Danger was around them—no, danger was waiting for them in North Dakota. What promise did she have that there would even *be* a future for her and Mac? Why not savor the time with him now?

Why not let all control go? It was so tempting.

Her hips pushed down on his, and Elizabeth rocked against the long length of his arousal. Again and again, her body rippled against his. She needed the pleasure they shared.

She needed him.

His hands clenched around her waist as he stared up at her. *Intent. Focused.* He'd never looked more so than in that moment. His green eyes glittered at her. "Just how long," Mac asked her, "do you really think my control will last?"

She needed to stop. But a fierce desire had taken hold of her. The girl she'd been—the one who'd lived in the moment, the one who'd felt alive when she took risks— that girl hadn't died. No matter how hard Elizabeth had tried to quiet her over the years, she was still there.

And she wanted out.

No, she wanted Mac.

She caught the lobe of his ear with her teeth and gave him a little lick. When a shudder rocked through him, a wave of sensual power filled Elizabeth. Mac was—

He lifted her off him. She nearly stumbled because he'd moved so fast. Her hand flew out to brace herself, but her fingers just tangled with his. "Come on," Mac ordered, and he pulled her toward the back of the plane. There was a small, separate area back there. He yanked aside the curtain, and she turned back to him, her body still aching and sensitive.

"You can't make a sound." His hands went to the snap of her jeans. "Neither will I. Because you're mine—everything that happens here is ours. Not for anyone else."

That wildness pumped harder in her. She'd tried to be someone else for so long. *I'm not perfect. And I hate always having control.*

She kicked her shoes aside and ditched her jeans.

Elizabeth reached for her underwear. Staring into his blazing eyes, she pushed the underwear down her legs and let it puddle at her feet.

Mac pulled her into his arms. He lifted her up easily. His strength could really be phenomenal. His arms were tight bands around her, and their gazes locked.

His arousal pushed against her. He'd opened his jeans, and that heavy length met her bare flesh.

"I'm protected," Elizabeth whispered. That part of her that never took chances—that side had made sure that her birth control was covered.

"I'm clean." His words were a rough rasp. "You don't have to worry."

She kissed him. Elizabeth let her tongue slide just inside his mouth in a sensual temptation. Part of her knew she should pull back. That she was opening a dangerous door inside herself that she wouldn't be able to close again.

But a bigger part of her didn't care.

"Then what are you waiting for?" Elizabeth whispered.

He lifted her up higher, positioned his body and surged into her.

Mac kissed her, hard and deep, so there was no sound for her to make. She was too far gone to do anything but hold on tight and ride out that wave of pleasure. Not easy. Not light. Shattering. Every thrust and glide of his body sent desire pulsing hotter and harder inside her. She was nearly clawing at his shoulders as Elizabeth fought to get closer to him. He controlled their movements perfectly, sliding her down so that each glide of his body worked over her sensitive core.

The climax was close, building at breakneck speed.

Her breath was heaving out, and the pleasure was going to hit. Elizabeth knew it—

Her breath choked out when the release hit her. It was so strong that her whole body seemed to spasm. And Mac was right there with her. She could feel him, inside and out, and her hold tightened on him.

The pleasure bound them, not just the flesh, but cutting far deeper.

Her breath was still coming in pants as she stared up at him. No one had ever made her feel the way he did.

His hands were still around her waist, and his eyes were locked on hers. What did he see in her gaze? Pleasure? Need?

Hope?

Her legs were clamped around his hips. She should move them. She should probably try to get some of her careful control back in place but...

She kissed his neck. "I don't have to hide with you, do I?"

His hand slid up her back. "No."

Elizabeth realized that Mac saw her for exactly who she was—controlled and wild. He wanted her, all of her.

"Do you do this a lot?" Elizabeth wondered, hating the question and the sudden jealousy that rose within her. "Have sex with women in—"

"No." A flat, hard denial.

Her lips curved, and her legs finally slid down. He lowered her gently to the floor. Mac adjusted his clothes, and she tried to hurriedly make sure she was somewhat back to normal.

Will the others know? Do I even care?

Right then, no, she didn't. When you were living

in the moment, you didn't get to worry so much about what others would think.

"Something you should understand…" Mac said, and his fingers caught hers. "I meant what I told you before. I don't want to let you go."

A shiver slid over her. She wished that she could see into his mind—his heart.

"What would it take," he continued, "to get you to stay with me?"

In that instant, Elizabeth decided that there would be no more lies or secrets. She wouldn't be afraid, not any longer. "You'd have to love me," Elizabeth told him simply. She watched his pupils flare. "More than anything else." Because she wasn't going to accept anything less.

No more fear. Happiness—life. Hope. The girl she'd been and the woman she'd become were tangled together now, and neither was going to hold back.

"How do you know," Mac asked, tilting his head to the side, "that I don't already?"

She nearly choked. "You—"

"Mac!" It was Sullivan's voice, sounding a bit too close. "We're going to be landing soon. You and Elizabeth need to buckle up again."

Landing? They were already there?

"Mac!"

Buckle up, right. That was what they were supposed to do and *not* have hot, passionate sex at thirty thousand feet.

Mac brought her hand to his lips. "Think about it," he told her. Then he pushed back the curtain.

She caught a glimpse of Sullivan's back. He was heading toward the cockpit once more. Had the guy realized what they'd been doing?

Hurrying now, she sat in her seat and reached for the seat belt. As it clicked into place, Elizabeth wondered just what it would be like if Mac loved her.

"WHAT THE HELL is going on with you?" Sullivan caught Mac's arm before he could leave the plane.

Mac didn't look at his brother. Instead, he kept his gaze on Elizabeth. She'd already disembarked, and the wind had caught her hair, tossing it around her face.

"This isn't you." Sullivan's grip hardened. "Since when do you get so caught up in a woman that you decide to scr—"

"Stop." Low. Lethal. "Be very, very careful when you talk about Elizabeth."

Sullivan's hand fell away. "You're in too deep with her. You have to watch your back. You can't trust—"

He finally looked at his brother. "She isn't Celia."

Sullivan actually flinched. "You know I don't talk about her."

"Maybe you should." He'd kept quiet for too long. "You know she helped save your ass back then. You were always so sure she'd betrayed you—*why?*"

Sullivan shouldered past him and exited the plane.

But Mac wasn't done. He followed his brother and grabbed his shoulder, swinging him back around. "I contacted her before we left," he said flatly.

Sullivan stared at him in shock.

"You need to deal with it," Mac said. He hadn't warned his brother because he'd known just how Sullivan would react. Too bad. They needed Celia on this one. "She should be in the airport, waiting for us. She was already in the area, working another case, so she was able to make the rendezvous I proposed."

His brother paled. "You had no right—"

"Celia is *my* connection, too. She's the one who set up the meeting with the governor. She was the only agent in the field who could do it for me. He doesn't know about Elizabeth or who I am. Celia pulled strings, and the guy just thinks he's meeting a few constituents after some fund-raiser. You know she has ties that will—"

"Don't."

He'd never heard that level of fury in Sullivan's voice.

"Mac?" Elizabeth called. "Is everything all right?" She began to walk toward them.

Mac stepped closer to his brother. "I understand now," he told him softly. "I didn't before. I didn't get why you changed so completely. Why you seemed so hard and brittle. I thought it was because the mission had gone bad."

Sullivan's eyes burned with his rage.

"But it was because you knew you'd lost her, wasn't it? You thought—"

"There are some things you can't undo," Sullivan gritted.

"And there are some things that you can." He didn't want Sullivan to keep being a shell of the man he'd been before. So bitter and angry. "I am getting in too deep with Elizabeth, just the way you did with Celia, right? But I'm not going to make the same mistakes you did. I'm going to trust *her*, the same way you should have trusted Celia when all the chips were down."

"You don't know anything about me and Celia. You don't—"

Elizabeth put her hands between them. "Are you two all right?"

Mac forced a smile for her. "Just trying to make my brother here see reason, before it's too late."

Sullivan retreated a step. "It's already too late. You can't change the past, no matter what you do." He whirled away from them and headed for the small airport.

"No." Elizabeth's voice was strong. "You can't. But that doesn't mean you have to remain stuck in the past or that you have to make the same mistakes."

Sullivan hesitated.

"We can all change," Elizabeth said. "It's not too late for any of us."

Sullivan glanced toward the airport, and the longing on his face was almost painful to see. Mac understood so much more about his brother now.

Sullivan had loved Celia, but he'd turned his back on her. He'd lost the one woman who truly made him happy.

Mac's gaze slid to Elizabeth. *What would I do if I lost her?* He'd been dead serious with her before. He knew exactly how he felt. He loved Elizabeth, and he'd prove that to her. When this mess was over, they'd start fresh. He'd take her out for drinks. He'd wine her, he'd dine her and he'd show her just what they could have together.

And if he was a particularly lucky SOB, she might just start to love him back.

"Why does he look as if he's heading toward a firing squad?" Elizabeth asked softly as her shoulder brushed against his. She tucked her hair behind her ear.

"Because he is," Mac said, and he caught her fingers in his. "So let's go give the poor guy some backup." It wasn't going to be easy for Sullivan to see Celia, for him to work with her again, but there was no choice.

Celia James had more ties to Uncle Sam than anyone else that Mac knew. She'd been able to arrange this little meeting in mere minutes. They needed her.

Too bad for them all... Sullivan had never admitted that he loved her.

Chapter Eleven

A woman with short red hair waited just inside the airport terminal. Her skin was a warm gold, and her eyes were a bright blue.

Her eyes were also currently locked on Sullivan.

Elizabeth slipped inside the airport with Mac, and she realized that Sullivan had come to a dead stop just a few feet away from the redhead. The tension between the two was so thick and hot that Elizabeth figured the temperature in the whole building must be rising.

"Hello, Sullivan," the woman said quietly, her voice calm. "You're looking well."

He opened his mouth to reply and then just stopped.

The redhead's brows rose. "Sullivan?"

He still wasn't speaking.

The woman straightened her shoulders and strode toward Elizabeth. She offered her hand. "I'm Celia James."

"No," Sullivan finally muttered. "You're not."

Celia glanced over at him, frowned, then focused on Elizabeth once more. "Sullivan is as charming as ever, I see." Her smile held the faintest edge of sadness. "I'm here to help."

Sullivan crept closer to her, but Celia didn't glance

his way. "I have a vehicle waiting outside for us. The governor should be wrapping up his fund-raiser in—" she glanced down at her watch "—the next forty-five minutes. When he gets to his house, he's expecting to find private donors waiting to meet him. You will be those donors."

Elizabeth's heart raced in her chest. "How did you make these arrangements?"

"His campaign manager owed me." Her smile turned cold. "But when Martin Pace finds out I'm actually here as part of a takedown on his boss, I don't think he's going to be thrilled that he repaid the debt."

"Thank you," Elizabeth said.

Celia's face softened. "Mac briefed me on your case. I'm sorry you had to face this mess alone all those years ago. I know what it's like when no one has your back."

Sullivan swore. "Celia…"

"But you can count on Mac now," Celia added as she cut her gaze toward him. "He never let me down."

"I'm *in* the damn room," Sullivan growled. "You could always just try stabbing me with that knife you like to keep strapped to your ankle. It would be a lot faster."

But it seemed that Celia didn't have anything to say to him now. "The car is waiting," she said again. "Ready?"

Elizabeth straightened her shoulders. "Past ready." It was time to face the monster. Time to get justice for Nate.

ALL TOO SOON, Celia was braking the SUV in front of a large estate home. Elizabeth had remained tense during the drive, because they'd gone straight through Gibson, her old town, and headed out to the country to find the governor's home.

Time had changed the little town of Gibson, and for the better. The old buildings were gone. New businesses had sprung up in their place. The whole area looked different, brighter.

Or maybe it had just been darker in her memory.

"Sutherfield keeps his estate home here," Celia said as she turned off the engine. "But he spends most of his time at the governor's mansion. We got lucky that he was out here for that fund-raising visit...we were able to cut through a lot of red tape."

She hurried out of the car. Elizabeth and the men followed her.

They'd had to pass through a large metal gate in order to get access to the mansion. But the guards at the gate hadn't hesitated when Celia had given them her ID. Apparently, the governor's campaign manager had told the guards that Celia and her guests were to be ushered right through security.

Just as they reached the front door, a tall, brown-haired man appeared. He stood on the threshold and looked somewhat nervously at Celia.

"Martin!" She gave him a hug. "Thanks for setting this up."

He cast a nervous glance at their little group. "They want to donate to the governor's vice-presidential run?" He appeared highly doubtful. Probably because they were all wearing jeans, and both Mac and Sullivan looked seriously dangerous as they glared at the guy. "Celia, what's—"

She pulled away from him. "Do you trust me?"

From the corner of her eye, Elizabeth noticed that Sullivan's hands fisted.

Martin nodded, a bit cautiously.

"Good, then believe me when I say that you don't want to be here tonight. You want to start distancing yourself from the governor."

He backed up a step. "What has he done?"

Since this guy was the campaign manager, then maybe he knew about the governor's dirty little secrets. Elizabeth stepped forward. "Does the name Nate Daniels mean anything to you?"

"No." Martin shook his head. "Should it?" He yanked a hand through his hair. "As soon as you called me, Celia, I got this knot in my gut… I knew this was going to be trouble…"

"I don't cause trouble," Celia said smoothly. "I eliminate it. You know that."

His hand dropped to his side. "I don't know Nate Daniels."

Celia seemed to consider that. "We think the governor knows him."

Martin turned and strode into the house. They followed him in, and Elizabeth's shoes squeaked against the marble floor. The place was immaculate inside—it even smelled expensive. She thought about Nate, about how he'd just had that old car and his beat-up jacket. How he'd smiled and said they'd start fresh.

All while his father sat in his mansion. Life wasn't fair. Not even close.

"He's making a bid for the White House," Martin said as he began to pace. "You know his name has been tossed around as a potential vice-presidential candidate. All of the plans are in motion. He and his wife,

Evelyn, have been working toward this goal for years. Do you have any idea, *any*, how much they've sacrificed for this?"

She remembered Nate's grave. All of the blood in that cabin. "I have an idea," Elizabeth said, her voice heating with the fury that burned in her.

Martin stopped pacing.

"This is your chance to leave," Celia said again. "You really want to take it. You don't want to go down with a sinking ship."

He blanched. "That bad?"

It was Mac who stepped forward. "We believe the governor has ties to a hit man who was recently arrested in Austin, Texas."

"*That* bad." Martin was sweating. His widening eyes locked on Mac. "Are you a cop?"

"PI," Mac said.

"We both are," Sullivan added darkly.

A furrow appeared between Martin's brows. "But… but if the governor did something wrong, shouldn't the cops be here?"

"The confession will come first," Celia said. She looked and sounded confident. Totally in control. "Then the cops. I'm all the authority that's needed right now."

"You're CIA…or is it FBI?" Martin appeared pained. "How the hell do I keep track of all the things you do these days? *A hit man!* How could he be so dumb? I mean, yeah, the guy might not be the most ethically sound fellow out there. He likes the ladies, and he's strayed a few times over the years, but it was nothing serious. Nothing *criminal.* He never even thought of leaving his wife. Well, except with that one girl…" His voice trailed away. "But that was long before my time with the governor. I just—I found a picture of them once. Evelyn saw it and told me that he'd nearly made a fatal mistake. But that the governor had come to his senses in time."

Had he? Or had he just *fixed* his mistake?

"You don't have much time," Celia told him. "I've called others in…"

"Press?" Martin demanded. "Or police?"

"Does it matter?"

He strode for the door. "Just let me know when it's all over…" And he didn't look back. Martin slammed the door behind him as he hurried out.

"He's going to warn his boss," Sullivan snapped. "That's obvious. He's going to tell the governor that we're here, and the guy is just going to stonewall us."

Celia glanced over at him. "Have a little faith…"

His eyelids flickered.

"Martin might work for the governor, but the guy doesn't own his soul. He won't talk."

"You're so sure of him." Sullivan stalked toward her. "Why? Are you involved with the guy?" His left hand carried a small black briefcase, but his right lifted, as if he'd touch Celia.

Elizabeth rubbed her forehead. "Look, whatever is going on with you two…" And plenty obviously was. "Just stop it, okay? The governor will be here soon and we need to be ready."

Celia nodded. "Right. Come this way." She motioned to the right. "His study is in here. The governor knows me, so I'll greet him at the door. I'll also make sure that no one interrupts us once we get started."

Celia was certainly an interesting woman.

Mac followed Elizabeth into the study. Sullivan was right on their heels.

"We need the guy to slip up," Sullivan said as he took up a post near the window. "When he makes a mistake, that's when we have him." He still had the briefcase in his hands.

"And by coming here, by catching him off guard, we immediately put the guy at a disadvantage," Mac added.

Elizabeth studied him for a moment. "Why do I get the feeling you've done your share of interrogations?"

"Because Uncle Sam trained me well." His stare was solemn. "I know how to spot lies. I know how to see the truth. The interrogations I did were in some hellholes, places I wish I could forget, but I learned valuable lessons there." He peered over at Sullivan. "We both did."

Sullivan's shoulders stiffened. "I wish I could forget some of those places, too."

"And some of the people?" Celia asked softly as she headed for the door.

"Not—" Sullivan began.

But Celia had left the room.

"Not you," he finished. "Not you, C."

Mac crossed to Elizabeth's side. "Are you ready for this?"

"Yes." Ready for it to be over. "If he's the one who sent that hit man after me...if he's done *all* of this—" her shoulders straightened "—then I'm ready to nail him to the wall."

"Bloodthirsty, isn't she?" Sullivan muttered.

Her angry stare flew toward him. "He's destroyed my life. He took away the man I loved."

Mac stiffened.

"Then he came after me again," Elizabeth's words

tumbled out. "Just when I was safe. Just when I felt like I might have found a place to stay, he started hunting me. He put Grant in danger. He put Mac in danger." Her chin jerked up. "That's not going to happen again. He has to pay for his crimes. We have to stop him before anyone else is hurt."

She heard voices out in the foyer. Celia. A man. A woman. Had the governor arrived?

"Showtime," Mac murmured.

Yes, it was.

Elizabeth braced herself. Mac was at her side, standing close. Sullivan kept his position near the window. The voices drew closer. A woman was laughing, a light, tinkling sound that grated on Elizabeth's nerves.

Then Celia was in the doorway. "Your guests are just in here, Governor," she murmured. "I hope you don't mind that I brought them inside."

The governor strode in behind her. He was tall, with broad shoulders. He was still wearing a tux, and in her jeans, Elizabeth suddenly felt terribly out of place.

Get a grip. He's a killer.

The governor glanced at her and smiled.

For a moment the world slowed down. The governor had one dimple in his left cheek. A dimple that flashed when he smiled. And his eyes were a deep gold. Very distinct.

"Hello, ma'am, gentlemen." The governor nodded to them all as his wife followed him into the room. She was dressed in a form-fitting blue gown, one that had a long slit that showcased her well-toned legs. Her hands were covered in white gloves that ended just below her elbows. The governor's wife was an attractive woman, perfectly styled, and she was giving their little group a practiced, polite smile.

"I'm so glad you wish to support my campaign," he began.

"You have his smile," Elizabeth blurted. She rubbed her suddenly pounding temples. "Or he had yours, I guess." Her head tilted to the side as she studied him. "The eyes are the same, too. I thought only Nate had eyes like that."

The governor paled. "I don't know what you're talking about."

"Yes," Mac said, taking an aggressive step forward. "You do, Governor. You know exactly what—or who—she's talking about." He glanced toward Sullivan.

Sullivan strode forward and placed his briefcase on the governor's desk.

"Wesley?" The governor's wife wrapped her fingers around his arm. "What's going on? Are these people here to support you?"

"No, Evelyn." His voice had thickened, and his shoulders had slumped a bit. "I don't think they are."

Evelyn's eyes turned cold and angry in a flash. "Then what's going on? Who are all of you?" She glanced over her shoulder. "Where's Martin? Didn't he set this up? Where's—"

"Is that you in the picture, Governor?" Sullivan asked.

He'd taken some photos out of the briefcase. He put one photo on the desk—it was the photo that Elizabeth and Mac had retrieved from Yeldon's place. The photo of a lone man at Nate's grave.

A man who looked a whole lot like the governor.

Wesley's fingers shook as he reached out to touch that photo.

"I think that is you," Mac said. He nodded to Sullivan, and another photo was placed on the desk. "And I think you know exactly who Nate Daniels is."

Elizabeth pressed her lips together. The photo Sullivan had just put on that desk showed Nate at the crime scene. It showed all the blood. It showed his body, exactly where it had fallen after his attack.

A shudder ran over Wesley's whole body.

"How did you do it?" Elizabeth asked. "How did you set up your own son's murder?"

Wesley's gaze whipped toward her. "What? No, no, I didn't!"

"Wesley!" Evelyn grabbed his arm and yanked him away from the desk. "You're being set up!" She gave him a hard shake. "These people must be reporters—they're trying to destroy us! Don't say another word." She pointed toward the door. "I want you all out of my house right this moment. If you don't leave, I will be calling the cops."

"The cops sound like a great idea to me," Celia said, nodding. "And they're already on their way. I had to contact the right ones, of course, a few detectives I know who weren't particularly impressed by your husband's position." She leaned forward and said, her voice hushed but carrying, "They didn't vote for him in the last election."

Evelyn's cheeks flushed a bright red. "You were supposed to be his ally! You came into our lives with the highest recommendation! You were CIA—"

"I came into your lives because you were already under investigation," Celia fired back. "There were some financial discrepancies that had been brought to my boss's attention. I've been watching the governor for quite some time. My boss wanted me to investigate, and then when the McGuires contacted me, well, let's just say that vanishing money suddenly made a whole lot more sense. When you're paying off a hit man, it takes a lot of cash, doesn't it? It's not like he'd be the type to accept credit."

"What are you talking about?" Wesley stumbled toward Celia. "I haven't hired any hit man! And I certainly never arranged for Nate's murder!" His voice dropped. "My son...*my son*..."

"Shut up," Evelyn ordered. "They'll use this against us! It will be in every tabloid in the country, and we will never sit in the White House!"

Wesley cut her a quick glance then nodded.

"Get out," Evelyn ordered again. "If the cops really are coming, they'd better have a warrant or they won't get past my front door."

Sullivan collected the photographs.

Celia inclined her head. "If that's the way you want to play it..."

Wait, were they really all just going to leave?

Elizabeth rushed toward the governor and she grabbed his arm. "Nate was a good man."

He blinked at her.

"He loved me." She'd never doubted that. "He had a beautiful smile and big dreams. And I know that all of his dreams would have come true. He was *good*," she said again. "I saw him empty his pockets to help someone else that he thought was worse off than he was. The whole time I was with him, he never complained about *anything*. He just talked about the good things that were coming." Her heart was breaking all over again. "He didn't get any of those good things." Tears slid down her cheeks. "Because you had him killed. You had your own son killed!"

"No!" His voice was hoarse. "I didn't… I didn't even find out about him until he was dead. I didn't know, I swear!"

"I'm calling security," Evelyn announced as she marched toward the desk and reached for the phone there. "You got past the team at the gate because you fed them your lies. They'll drag you all out now."

Mac stepped forward. "If you didn't kill him, Governor, then why won't you talk to us? Why won't you answer our questions?"

"This is Evelyn," the governor's wife snapped into the phone. "I need security at the main house right now. We have intruders here that must be escorted off the property immediately."

"Like this is the first time we've ever been kicked out of a place," Sullivan rasped, a rough grin sliding over his face.

Elizabeth glanced away from Sullivan and back at the governor. He was staring at her with wide eyes.

"I…know you," Wesley said. "I saw you at Nate's funeral."

Her heart slammed into her ribs. *This is it!* "Yes, you did."

"Did you…did you really love my son?"

Elizabeth nodded.

Mac was silent, watching. The only person in that room who *wasn't* silent was Evelyn. She was barking orders, screaming for the security team to get there.

"I wish I'd known him," Wesley confessed. "I—I

got his letter to me, saying that he was coming, but he never showed up."

And she remembered what the hit man had said, *Look what happened to Nate! He should have just kept driving! Another hour and I never would've been able to touch him, but he screwed up.*

"He was coming to see you," she said, struggling to put the puzzle pieces together. "But then he met me."

Wesley shook his head. "I don't—"

"He told me that he'd let his past go the day that he met me." She swiped at her cheeks. "He wasn't going to ruin your career! He wasn't going to create some kind of scandal. He let it all go." Pain squeezed her heart. "Why couldn't you let it go, too?" It hurt to stare into eyes so like Nate's. "Why did you have to kill him?"

The governor's hands latched around her shoulders, holding tight. "I didn't!" He shook her. "I didn't!" His voice rose. "I would never—"

Mac grabbed him and tossed the guy back against the desk. "You don't hurt her." His hands were fisted and ready to attack. "You don't put your hands on her, you understand? Try it again and you'll see just how violent I can truly become."

Even Evelyn was silent.

"I'm sorry," Wesley said as he pressed his hands to his eyes. "It's just—seeing those pictures. Seeing him like that." His hands dropped, and he tried to meet Elizabeth's stare, but Mac stood in front of her, shielding her with his body. "Did he suffer? Did he cry out? Did he say anything at the end?"

Elizabeth bit her lip so hard she was surprised she didn't taste blood. "He screamed," she told him starkly as she moved to Mac's side. "He told me to run. With his last breath, he was saving me."

The lines on Wesley's face seemed to deepen. "I didn't know. I found his letter *after* he was already gone. I had an assistant back then. She'd opened it and thought it was some kind of blackmail threat. She didn't even tell me about it. Not until it was too late."

He was really going to stand there and lie to them?

"I don't believe you," Elizabeth said flatly. "You hired that hit man to kill Nate. And then you hired the same man to come after me in Austin." Her pounding heartbeat shook her chest. "He's dead now, by the way. Your *Fixer* was killed when he tried to escape from police custody."

"He…came after you?"

Mac was still standing protectively close. Did he think the governor was going to attack her?

"You've been the governor here for so long. People love you." Disgust twisted her lips. "But they don't really know you, do they? Yes, the killer came for me. And he also came for a reporter named Steve Yeldon. I was lucky. I lived, thanks to Mac and his brothers."

Mac caught her fingers in his.

"Steve wasn't so lucky," she continued. "The Fixer stabbed him in a dirty alley and left him to die."

Wesley's body shuddered.

Evelyn put the phone back down. She hurried to her husband's side. "His heart is weak! He doesn't need this stress." She wrapped her arms around him. *"Get out."*

Elizabeth turned for the door. She'd wanted a confession. Wanted proof. She'd stared the monster in the eyes and she'd seen—

Pain. *Pain* had stared back at her.

The governor must be one fine actor, because that grief and horror on his face had looked real, too.

She heard the front door crash open, and a thunder of footsteps raced toward the study.

"That would be the guards," Sullivan said, voice wry, "coming to drag us out."

Sure enough, the guards burst in. One immediately grabbed for Celia.

Sullivan lunged forward. "You need to watch that." His voice was lethal. "That's no way to handle a lady." His fingers flexed, as if he was getting ready to deliver a punch.

"Don't hurt them," the governor ordered. His voice seemed low, weak. "They were just leaving."

Like she wanted his protection. Elizabeth strode for the door, but then she glanced back at him. "Did you kill his mother, too?"

The governor stared at her in confusion, but beside him, Evelyn's mouth dropped in shock. For just an instant, she let go of her husband's arm.

"Nate's mother. She was killed in a hit and run when he was just a little kid." Now she was going with her gut. "Another job for the Fixer, huh? I guess he's been on the payroll for a long time."

Mac's shoulder brushed against her. "That Fixer of yours talked to the cops. Got real chatty with Detective Ben Howard. Trust me, you won't be getting away with anything that you've done." He gave a mocking salute. "We'll be seeing you again real soon, Governor."

The guards were all around them, all dressed in black and glancing a bit nervously at the governor and his wife.

The guards didn't touch them again, not as they

slowly walked out of the mansion. Elizabeth didn't hear the shriek of any police cruisers approaching, so she wondered if Celia's story about the cops had just been BS to stall while they questioned the governor.

"That was certainly interesting," Celia murmured as they neared the SUV.

Sullivan caught her arm. "Did he hurt you?"

She laughed. "Really, Sully? You know it takes a whole lot more than that to *hurt* me." Her voice sharpened. "You—of all people—know that I don't break."

Mac opened the SUV's passenger door. Elizabeth started to climb in.

"Wait!"

The desperate cry had Elizabeth glancing back. Evelyn was running toward her, her gown tripping up her legs, and her face a frantic mask. "Wait! Miss— I didn't even get your name!"

Elizabeth turned toward her. "Elizabeth Snow."

The woman staggered to a stop in front of her. She glanced nervously at the others then said, "We have to talk. You and I…alone."

"The hell you do," Mac said immediately. "If you've got something to say, then just say it right here in front of us all."

Evelyn's gloved hands twisted together. "He's…he's got a temper, you see." Her breath heaved out. "I lived with him all these years… *I've* witnessed it." And she didn't look so confident and cold any longer. Instead, her face had twisted with fear, and her eyes held dark shadows. "That boy's mother…you mentioned that you ̇ought my husband had killed her, too?"

̇nd Elizabeth remembered the way Evelyn had

pulled away from the governor when she'd dropped that particular bombshell.

"We sure think that's a possibility," Mac said grimly. "A very strong possibility."

"Was her name—" her eyes squeezed shut "—Gloria?"

Elizabeth's heart stopped. "Yes! Yes!" Elizabeth stepped closer to the other woman. "He told you about her?"

"She...she was one of his mistakes." Her lips trembled. "So many over the years, but I remember her because one night...he was having a nightmare. He screamed her name. When I asked about her, he told me later that...Gloria was a problem that he'd fixed."

Her heart was racing again, but it sure seemed as if a cold wind had just wrapped tightly around her. Elizabeth shivered.

Evelyn glanced over her shoulder. "I've lived with him so long. He *was* a good man, once..." Her voice trailed away.

"You need to come with us," Elizabeth said immediately. "Come with us to the police, and you can tell us everything you know."

But Evelyn backed up. "I can't turn on my husband."

Mac swore. "He's a killer! So his hands didn't get dirty, so what? He ordered those deaths! And how do you know that he won't decide to do the same to you?"

Evelyn shook her head. "No, you're wrong—"

But Sullivan had joined them, and he brutally asked, "If you're no longer useful to him, how long do you really think he'll keep you around?"

The guards spilled out of the house. "Ma'am? Is there a problem?" one of them called.

Her eyes were stark as she backed away. "No problem. They're leaving."

"Evelyn," Elizabeth said, "help us."

But Evelyn turned away and headed back into the house.

Chapter Twelve

"Where was the backup?" Sullivan demanded when Celia pulled the SUV up in front of a small hotel. "I thought you said detectives were coming in, riding to the rescue."

Mac noted the edge in his brother's voice. Sullivan didn't have his normal control in place, not by a long shot. But then, where Celia was concerned, the guy never did.

"You guys didn't give me enough evidence to bring in any detectives." Celia killed the engine. "I was hoping we'd rattle the governor enough for him to slip up."

They all exited the vehicle, but no one moved to approach the hotel. It was a small place, one of those little spots that most people passed right by as they headed on to look for something bigger and better.

"He did slip up," Elizabeth said, voice subdued. "He admitted he was at Nate's funeral. He got a note from Nate. He thought Nate was blackmailing him."

When a tremble slid over her, Mac wrapped his arms around Elizabeth and pulled her close.

"No," Celia said, sighing, "he was careful. He just said that his *assistant* thought Nate was working some kind of blackmail scheme. The governor did a good job of looking shocked and horrified, but he didn't give us anything to actually use against him."

Elizabeth slid a bit closer to Mac. "The wife is our key. She knows so much more than she's saying. We just have to get her to open up to us."

Sullivan nodded. "We have to get the woman to turn on her husband. *Not* the easiest task. Because when he goes down, her world will explode with him."

"Crash and burn," Mac muttered. But yes, that was exactly what they would have to do—they'd have to get Evelyn to expose the governor.

"Who knows a man better," Sullivan mused as he stalked closer to Celia, "than the woman he's sleeping with?"

"Sully…" Mac warned. "Watch yourself."

Sullivan stopped.

"I'll go get some rooms," Celia announced. "Be right back." Then she was hurrying off—nearly running—for the little check-in office and its bright vacancy sign.

Sullivan watched her go. It was dark out there, with the stars partially obscured by clouds, so Mac couldn't see his brother's expression clearly.

"What happens next?" Elizabeth asked. "We came all this way… What do we do? I can't just walk away from this."

No, and he didn't expect her to do that. "Next, we sleep. We rest. Then when the sun comes up again, we're going to start working on that weak link." *On Evelyn.* He turned Elizabeth in his arms so that he could face her. "This isn't over, not by a long shot. You need to believe me on that. I'm not giving up."

"I do believe you." Her hand rose and slid against his cheek. Her touch was so soft. Meanwhile, he had rough stubble on his cheeks. He always felt too rough around her. "Thank you."

He turned his head and pressed a hot kiss to her palm. "Any damn time." *I'd do anything, for you.*

Sullivan was silent, but Mac could practically feel his brother stewing over there. He was sure that, as soon as they were alone, Sullivan was going to have plenty to say.

Yes, I brought in Celia. Yes, I know you think I just screwed up your whole damn life.

Celia ran back to them. "They only had three rooms."

Not a problem. "Elizabeth and I can share." They *would* share. Because he needed her in his arms again. Needed to feel her go wild beneath him. He liked it when Elizabeth let her control go. Hell, he liked everything about her.

Celia tossed a key to Elizabeth, then she threw one to Sullivan. He caught it easily, his fingers clenching around it.

"Our rooms are right next to each other," Celia told him. "Hope that's not a problem."

"Not a problem," Sullivan gritted. But he sure sounded as if it was the worst problem ever.

"I'll grab the bags," Mac said. "Celia and Elizabeth, why don't you two go ahead and see just how crappy the rooms are…" Mostly, he needed them to slide ahead so he could give his brother a warning.

He waited until the women were clear, then he closed in on Sullivan. "You need to watch yourself," Mac began.

Sullivan whirled toward him. "You don't even know what you've done." Each word vibrated with fury. "I tried to stay away from her. And *you*—you just brought her right back to me!"

As if that was a crime? "You need her—"

"Too much. That's the problem. You saw what I did to us both before. What the hell am I supposed to do now?" He stared down at his fisted hands. "How am I supposed to just let her walk away again?"

Mac hated his brother's pain. "Maybe you don't let her walk. Maybe you hold as tight to her as you can."

Sullivan's head shot up. "The way you're holding on to Elizabeth?"

The way I'm trying to hold her.

"Didn't you hear the way she talked about Nate?" Sullivan suddenly demanded. "How are you supposed to fight against that?"

Mac's stomach tightened. "Don't go there." *Because yeah, I heard.*

"She loved him. Loved him so much that years later, she's willing to risk her life to give him justice."

Mac could feel battle-ready tension sweeping through him.

"How do you handle that, Mac? How do you fight a ghost? You want her, but she loves *him*."

Too far. Mac grabbed the front of his brother's shirt and yanked the guy toward him. "Just because you shut yourself off, it doesn't mean that everyone else did, too."

"You're hooked on a woman who can't love you." Sullivan shoved at him, but Mac didn't let him go. "Is that some kind of punishment you're giving yourself? A new game of torture? Don't get closer to her. Don't give her any more of yourself."

Mac wanted to shake him. "You don't know what you're talking about."

"Yes, I do! Because I've been right where you are." And Sullivan tore away from Mac. "You love her, but she doesn't love you back, and it will *destroy* you if you let it. Pull back. Pull back before there is nothing left of you."

You love her. Those words hung in the air.

And so did Elizabeth's soft gasp.

THE GUARDS WERE GONE.

Evelyn Sutherfield walked slowly toward the study. The house was so quiet. Such a big, giant house. A place like that probably should have been filled with dozens of children.

She and Wesley had never had children.

Her gown trailed behind her as she paused at the entrance to Wesley's study. He loved that study. He often spent hours and hours locked away in there.

Wesley was in that study, right then. Sitting at his desk.

Evelyn wiped away the tear that slid down her cheek.

A gun had fallen to the floor beside her husband's favorite chair. And her husband's head—a bullet had slammed into it. His eyes were closed, his body slumped back and blood poured from the great, gaping wound that had been left behind.

She should call someone. She should do…*something*.

But Evelyn just stood there and stared at her husband's dead body.

SHE KNOWS.

"I—I came back to help with the bags," Elizabeth said, her voice hitching a bit as she stepped forward.

Sullivan swore. Then he glanced around a bit frantically. "Is Celia with you?"

"She went on into her room." Elizabeth was only a few feet from Mac. "Can you give us a minute alone?"

Mac needed more than a minute. He had to figure out a way to smooth things over.

"Sure thing." Sullivan hurried away, but then he paused and glanced back at Mac. "Sorry," he said stiffly. "You know I'm a jerk and I— *Just don't make my mistakes, man.* You don't want that hell."

Mac grabbed the bags from the back of the SUV and locked the vehicle. Then he turned and found Elizabeth right in his path.

"Do you love me?" Her question hung between them.

Mac tightened his hold on the bags. "Let's get inside." *And let me think of some way to handle this.* He didn't want Elizabeth to run from him, and if the woman figured out just how obsessed he was…hell, yes, she might put some distance between them.

Elizabeth didn't speak again, not when he dropped Celia's bag off at her door and or when he tossed a backpack at Sullivan. But as soon as they entered the room they were going to share…

"It was a simple question, Mac. You can respond with a yes or with a no." She locked the door and faced him. "Your brother seemed to think that you did love me."

"As my own brother admitted…" Mac dropped the remaining bags. "He can be a jerk. And Sullivan doesn't know nearly as much as he thinks."

She rocked back on her heels. "So you don't love me." She tucked her hair behind her ear. "I thought you—"

He stalked toward her. Elizabeth stopped talking and

stared up at him with her wide, gorgeous eyes. Deliberately, he put one hand up on either side of her body, caging her between him and the door. "You really want to know how I feel?"

"Yes," she whispered. "That's why I asked."

"Be sure, because there won't be any going back. You won't be able to pretend you don't know, and I won't be holding back with you any longer."

"I don't want you to hold back."

Damn but she was beautiful. "You loved him." Sullivan's words had burned, because the accusation about her loving Nate? Yeah, he knew it was true. "Will you ever get past that?"

A faint line appeared between her brows. "Nate was the first boy who touched my heart. He made me happy, and yes, I did love him."

Right. His hands shoved harder against that door.

"But that doesn't mean I can't love someone else." Her hand rose and pressed to his chest, right over his racing heart. "It doesn't mean that I don't already love someone else."

He was supposed to be confessing. But she—

"I don't want to go back. I want to go forward, with you." Elizabeth rose onto her toes, and her lips brushed against his. "You helped me to come alive again, Mac. You scared me, and you excited me and you—you trusted me."

Her hand was still over his heart, and that heart was sure drumming out of control.

"I don't know when I started to love you," Elizabeth said, her lips curling in that slow smile that always got to him. "I just know that I do. And I can't imagine my life without you in it. I don't want to imagine it."

His mouth crushed against hers. Euphoria rolled through him so fast and so hard. And—

Sully could be such an idiot.

He wasn't his brother. She wasn't Celia. And they would not be making the same mistakes.

"I can just be me with you. You accept me, just as I am." Her mouth brushed against his again. "How could I not love you?"

And how could he not love her? He was *insane* for her, and Mac scooped her up in his arms. He kissed her frantically, the desire in him surging to the surface. They fell on the bed, a tangle of limbs on those saggy mattresses, but he didn't care. He kept kissing her and touching her. He wanted her clothes off, and Mac wanted to be in her.

The here and now—that mattered. Their future together—*that* mattered.

He grabbed her T-shirt and yanked it over her head. The perfect mounds of her breasts pushed against her bra, and he kissed his way past the edge of lace. She arched toward him, and he slid his hand under her back, reaching for the clasp of that bra. He needed—

"Mac!" Sully's hand pounded on the door that connected their rooms. "We've got to go! Now!"

Now? *Now?* Mac looked up at Elizabeth's face. Her cheeks were flushed, her eyes glittering, her lips red and swollen from his kiss. He had her under him on that bed. There was no other place in the world that he wanted to *go* to right then.

"The governor's wife just called Celia—she wants us at the house. Right now." Sullivan's fist hit the door. "What the hell are you doing, man? Come on!"

Elizabeth's breath whispered out. "You think she changed her mind and decided to turn on him?"

He pushed away from her. Because if he didn't get away from her, Mac knew he would be taking Elizabeth. Simple fact. His hands were shaking with the effort of holding back, so he clenched them into fists. He sat on the edge of the bed and tried to yank back his control.

The bed dipped as Elizabeth moved closer. She wrapped her arms around him and kissed his neck. "This is a pause. We'll talk to the wife. Get her to help us stop the governor. And then we can be together again. Only there won't be anything else to interrupt us, nothing to stop us."

He caught her hand in his. "Nothing." He turned his head and met her gaze.

Elizabeth smiled at him.

Sullivan pounded on the door. "We're leaving! The woman was frantic, okay? Saying that we had to get there right *then.* Are you coming?"

"Remind me to kick his butt later, okay? Just for fun."

Her smile widened. "I'll remind you to make love with me later, just for fun."

Elizabeth.

She slid away from him, yanked on her shirt and hurried toward the connecting door. She pulled it open just before Sullivan could pound again.

Sullivan glared at Mac as he sat on the side of the bed. "What in the hell, man? What were you—"

Mac lifted his brows.

"Oh." Sullivan cleared his throat. "Right. Let's go." Then he hurried back into his room.

Mac rose and paced toward Elizabeth. She'd told

him, actually *said* that she loved him. He wanted to tell her how he felt, too. Only he didn't want to be racing away after he said those words. He wanted to sink into Elizabeth and hold her close.

"Nothing will stop us," he told her softly. *Because I won't let it.*

THE LIGHTS WERE blazing inside the governor's house, but...

There had been no security at the main gate, and when Elizabeth climbed out of the SUV with the others, she still saw no sign of any guards.

"The front door is open," Celia said. Worry laced her words. "That can't be good."

No, it didn't seem like a good thing. Cautiously, they all advanced toward the house.

At that open door, Celia paused. "Evelyn!" she called out. "Evelyn, where are you?"

"Here." Her voice drifted faintly to them from inside.

They crossed the threshold.

Elizabeth noted the tense expressions that Mac and Sullivan both wore. They were obviously expecting trouble. Only fair, since she was expecting the same thing.

"Stay close," Mac told her.

She nodded.

"Evelyn?" Celia shouted once more.

"In the study..."

Sullivan and Celia hurried toward the study. Elizabeth looked up, seeing the glittering chandelier above her. Where was the governor? Had all the guards been sent home?

"Dear God!" That shocked cry came from the study.

She could see Celia and Sullivan just inside the door-way. They appeared frozen.

She and Mac hurried after them. Mac pushed Sullivan to the side—and Elizabeth saw the governor.

"I found him like this," Evelyn said softly. Her left hand smoothed over the governor's shoulder. He still wore his tux. A very blood-stained tux. "I'd sent everyone away because we needed to talk, without so many eyes and ears on us. Then I heard the boom." Her right hand was behind the long length of her dress.

She had blood on her beautiful dress.

"I guess it's over now," Evelyn said. Her lashes lifted, and she stared at Elizabeth. "My husband is dead."

Yes.

"Is that what you wanted?" Evelyn asked her. "For him to suffer, for him to die?"

"No," Elizabeth said at once. "I didn't come here to kill him." She'd wanted him to go to jail, not end up like this.

"It's all over," Evelyn said. Her breath sighed out and her shoulders slumped. "Will anyone even remember the good he did? Or do people just focus on the bad?"

He killed his son. Sent a hit man after me. That's plenty bad.

"Can we just…end things here?" Evelyn was pleading with tears in her eyes. "Why drag this out? It doesn't have to leave this room. He paid for his crimes. Let… let everyone focus on the good." Now she was speaking so quickly, her words tumbling out. "If you go to the press, it will be a feeding frenzy. I can say—say it was an accident. He was cleaning his gun."

Elizabeth shook her head and stepped toward the grief-stricken woman.

"I can say he was depressed!" Evelyn's voice rose. "He was—he'd been seeing a shrink for years. Ever since that bitch Gloria died."

Elizabeth stiffened.

The tension in that room ratcheted up.

"Oh, dear..." Evelyn blinked away her tears. "I wasn't supposed to say that, was I?"

Then she lifted her right arm, the one that had been hiding behind her dress. Too late, Elizabeth saw the gun in the other woman's hand. Her white-gloved fingers easily held the weapon.

Evelyn fired, shooting straight at Elizabeth. The bullet slammed into her, and Elizabeth fell backward.

She hit the floor even as more gunfire raged. Thundering all around her.

"Mac!" She tried to push back to her feet. Had he been hit, too? What about Sullivan? Celia? "Mac?" Her voice didn't come out as a scream, more of a rasp.

And even though she was trying, Elizabeth couldn't get up. Not all the way. She managed to sit up, but that was it. She couldn't stand because she hurt too much.

Blood. All over me.

"Mac?" He was the one she needed.

"Don't worry about him," Evelyn said. Elizabeth looked up and saw the woman aiming the gun right at her head. "Worry about yourself."

Chapter Thirteen

"Put down the gun," Mac ordered, fighting to keep his voice calm when there wasn't a single calm thing about him. Evelyn had shot Elizabeth—*shot her!* And he'd watched in horror as Elizabeth fell.

Before he could run to Elizabeth's side, Evelyn had been firing in quick succession, shooting at Celia— hitting her. Firing at Mac and at Sullivan.

Mac's upper arm throbbed where the bullet had hit him, but that wound wasn't going to slow him down. He would be getting to Elizabeth.

Nothing will stop me.

Celia was on the floor, not moving, and Sullivan had pulled himself up to a sitting position. There was so much blood on his brother.

Evelyn isn't going to let any of us leave.

Evelyn laughed at him and put the gun against Elizabeth's forehead. "Didn't expect me to be a good shot, did you? But I've been hunting since I was a girl. I know my way around guns." She laughed again. "Though no one could miss from this close, right?"

He held up his hands, wincing as the pain in his left arm deepened. "Don't do it."

Evelyn stared into Elizabeth's eyes. "You don't seem

so hard to kill." Her head tilted. "Why did Nelson have so much trouble with you? It's an easy-enough matter to put a bullet between your eyes."

"N-Nelson?" Elizabeth whispered.

Evelyn nodded. "You met my Fixer, didn't you? Dear Nelson…he's been helping me for years."

Mac crept closer. He had to get near enough to take that gun away from Evelyn. "So it was you, all along? You, not your husband?"

Evelyn cast a scornful glance toward him. "That man never had an original idea of his own, not once in all the years of our marriage. Everything he's accomplished has been because of me."

A car engine growled, catching Mac's attention. Then he heard the slam of a door. "Someone's coming," he told Evelyn. "It's the police. You need to—"

"It's not the police. It's my cleanup crew."

Footsteps raced toward them. "Evelyn!" a male voice called out. "Tell me you—"

Mac knew that voice. He glanced over his shoulder and saw Martin Pace stumble to a stop just inside the study.

"Evelyn," Martin said in shock. "What the hell? I thought you were just going to shoot the governor!" He bent next to Celia and swore. "What did you do?" His fingers lingered against Celia's neck.

Mac cut a quick glance toward his brother. Sullivan was rising now, and it appeared he was about to lunge at the governor's campaign manager.

Not yet, Sully. Not yet. Because that gun was digging into Elizabeth's forehead. If they made one wrong move, Evelyn's finger would squeeze the trigger, and Elizabeth would be gone.

"I did what I had to do," Evelyn snapped. "And don't start acting like you're not just as involved as I am—with just as much to lose!"

Martin still had his fingers against Celia's throat. "It was just supposed to be the governor." He looked up at Evelyn, glaring. "You shot her!"

"And she sold us out! You told me that she didn't warn you about what was coming—that she just appeared with the McGuires in tow! You owe that woman no loyalty. I'm the one you owe! I'm the one with the power!"

"No," Elizabeth said softly, "you're just the killer."

Evelyn's hold tightened on the gun. "And you're just some dumb piece of trash who got in the way."

Mac took another step toward her. Rage nearly blinded him. "You think you're going to kill us all now, is that it?"

Evelyn shrugged. "The way I see it, my husband killed you. You found out that he'd hired a hit man, and he went crazy. *Boom.* He shot you. He shot you all, then he turned the weapon on himself. Fortunately, I was lucky enough to escape from his madness."

Sullivan was on his feet, waiting for a signal. Mac understood and tried to figure out just when they needed to attack. *I have to get Evelyn to move the gun.*

"You were worried that we'd connect you," Elizabeth said. She didn't sound afraid. Not even with that gun pointed at her forehead, she wasn't afraid. She was angry. "Or maybe your husband…did he make the connection? Is that what happened? When we left…did he confront you? Maybe he realized that *you* had also known about Nate's letter all those years ago."

"I didn't need the damn letter," Evelyn shouted. "I

had Nelson following my husband. He started as a PI. *My* PI. When he learned about Gloria and her brat, I offered him fifty thousand dollars cash to make that problem go away. And guess what? He did. He fixed that problem for me, just like he learned to fix problems for plenty of others. I'm the one who sent clients his way. I made him."

Mac had seen plenty of monsters over the years. They came in all shapes and sizes. Some of the most evil killers could hide so very well. "You hoped Nate would never figure out who his father was, right? But then you learned he was coming to meet the governor."

The gun lifted—just a bit—from Elizabeth's forehead. Elizabeth was sitting up, but her body had started to sway. Where had the bullet hit her? *Not near her heart. Please, not there.*

"Having an illegitimate child would have ruined *everything.*"

"No, learning that his wife had killed his mistress," Elizabeth whispered, "that would have ruined…everything. You were never trying to protect anyone…but yourself." Her words were weaker, and she trembled.

Mac tried to keep Evelyn's attention on him, not Elizabeth. "He realized the truth tonight. He was going to send you to prison, wasn't he? He was going to tell the world exactly what you are."

"It's all her fault!" Evelyn screamed. "She just wouldn't stop!" She was glaring at Elizabeth once more, and that gun barrel was flush against Elizabeth's skin again. "You wanted to find a connection between Nelson and Wesley… I was the only connection. You would

have exposed me! I wasn't made for jail. I wasn't made for a normal life. I was made for *more.*"

"You're…crazy," Elizabeth told her. "That's all you are."

Evelyn's smile was cold and cruel. "Martin, if Celia isn't already dead, then take out your gun and put a bullet in her heart."

"Wh-what?"

"You brought your gun, didn't you? Just like I asked?" She was still staring at Elizabeth. "Shoot Celia. Then kill the men. They won't move—they can't." Her head turned, and she met Mac's stare. "Soldiers. SEALs. Your family is full of protectors. And you won't attack, you will *protect,* right up until the last moment. You will do anything to try and save Elizabeth here. So you won't move. You'll just be slaughtered because you realize that I will pull the trigger—"

"You're…gonna pull it…no matter what…" Elizabeth gasped out the words.

"He loves you, fool that he is," Evelyn said, sounding smug and crazy and cold. "You don't risk the life of the person you love. So he won't move. He'll be a good soldier and follow orders…"

From the corner of his eye, Mac saw that Martin had a gun in his hand.

The time to act…it's now. Mac gave a small inclination of his head, knowing that Sullivan would see the movement. Evelyn was wrong about them. They weren't just good soldiers.

They were well-trained killers.

Time to let their darkness out.

Nothing will stop us.

"My brothers have the evidence," Mac said as he took an aggressive step forward. He was bluffing for all he was worth as he went on a hunch and said, "We'd already linked you to Gloria's death. You should never have gone down there to see her, but you just had to lay eyes on the woman who nearly ruined your perfect dreams."

Evelyn's jaw dropped. "How did you—"

She did go see her.

"You're lying! You have proof of nothing!"

"My brothers are going to contact Steve Yeldon's reporter friends. They're going to run the story on you. *You'll* be the one who's dead—dead in the media. In politics. You'll rot in jail, and there will be no *more* for you."

"No!" Evelyn screamed, and her rage made her reckless. She yanked the gun away from Elizabeth and pointed it at Mac. "You—"

She was squeezing the trigger.

But Elizabeth surged up and slammed into her. Both women crashed onto the floor. Mac leaped forward and pulled Elizabeth back even as Evelyn brought up her gun once more.

He was faster than Evelyn. He knocked the gun away before she could fire, and then Elizabeth slammed her fist into Evelyn's face.

Evelyn fell back, and her head hit the side of the desk.

"Drop that gun," Sullivan ordered, his voice a low snarl. "Drop it and get the hell away from Celia."

Mac whirled around. Martin stood over Celia's body and he had the gun in his hand, but he wasn't pointing it at her. He'd aimed the weapon at Sullivan instead.

Mac kept his body in front of Elizabeth's. No one

would be getting another shot at her. *The bullet will have to go through me first.*

"This wasn't supposed to happen," Martin said, his words rushing out frantically. "I didn't… I didn't know what Evelyn was doing. I noticed that money was missing. I told her about it…then, hell, she paid me to keep quiet. I thought she might have a drug habit. I didn't know she was killing people!"

"You know now," Mac said flatly. "Drop the gun and get away from Celia."

Martin peered down at Celia. "I think she's already gone. I—I think—"

A cry of rage broke from Sullivan, and he launched at the other man, driving into him hard and fast. They slammed into the wall, and the gun fell from Martin's hand. Sullivan started pounding the guy, again and again.

"S-Sully…?" Celia's weak voice.

He froze. Then he dropped Martin and grabbed her, pulling her close. "We need an ambulance!" Sullivan yelled.

Mac felt Elizabeth's fingers on his back. He turned toward her—

And he caught her as she fell.

He was still holding her when the ambulance came, still cradling her tightly against him. But when the EMTs loaded Elizabeth onto the stretcher, her lashes opened and she whispered, "Nothing…nothing is going to stop us."

"Not a single thing," he vowed.

"I…love you."

And she damn well owned his soul.

Elizabeth smiled.

SHE HAD A SCAR. A nice, interesting battle wound. Evelyn Sutherfield had been arrested. The media was currently ripping her life apart.

Martin Pace had only been too happy to make a deal with prosecutors. Elizabeth knew he'd been talking pretty much constantly, and spilling every secret that he possessed.

Her nightmare was over. Nate had gotten his justice. She wasn't being hunted any longer.

There was nothing stopping her now.

Except Mac.

Elizabeth gazed out at the lake. Mac was being extremely problematic lately. They'd gotten home a few days ago, and he'd been in a rather überprotective mode. Sweet, in its way. Also…stifling, in its way.

The danger was over for them, and it was definitely time to move on.

"Elizabeth…"

She glanced to the left and saw Mac walking up the bluff toward her. The sun hit his dark hair and slid over the hard lines of his face. As always, a thrill shot through her when she saw him. Her heart beat a little faster. Her breath came a little quicker. And her smile spread slowly.

"Are you sure you feel up to being out here?" Mac asked her, frowning as he closed the distance between them. "The doctor said—"

"Stop." Because this had to end. "I'm okay, and you can't keep acting as if I'm going to collapse at any moment. I'm not. I'm fine." More than fine…if he'd just stop treating her with kid gloves! She missed his passion. His warmth.

Time to get their lives back on track.

"You scared me," Mac said, voice stark. "There was so much blood, and I knew the bullet had gone into your chest."

It had. But… "You heard the doctors. I'm lucky. My heart's fine—and so is everything else."

He brushed back the hair that blew across her cheek. "No," he told her starkly. "I'm lucky. Because if something had happened to you, I would've lost my mind." He swallowed, and his fingers gently caressed her cheek. "Do you have any idea how much I love you?"

She stared at him, waiting. *I'd really like to know.*

"I can't imagine a world without you in it, Elizabeth. I don't want to imagine one."

"I'm not going anyplace," she told him. *You don't have to know that world.*

"I know I can be overprotective—"

She raised her brows.

"I can be intense," he added. "And I tend to like adrenaline a bit too much."

Elizabeth waited.

"I would trade everything I have and everything I am in order to keep you safe. You matter more to me than anything." He pulled in a deep breath and dropped to his knee before her. Mac reached into his pocket.

"Mac…"

He offered her a ring. A beautiful diamond ring that sparkled in the sunlight. "My life is better when you're in it," he said simply. "Please, baby…will you do me the honor of marrying me?"

She saw it then, the hint of fear in his eyes. The nervousness that tightened his mouth. Her fierce warrior, waiting, hoping…

Did he think that she might say no?

Elizabeth pulled him to his feet. "My life is better," she told him softly, "when you're by my side." She kissed him. Loved him. "And yes, you wonderful man, I'll marry you."

He laughed and wrapped his arms around her. His laughter boomed out, so happy and free.

She kissed him again, totally lost and in love, safe and happy...

She could be wild with him. She could be controlled. She could be anything she wanted—and she knew that Mac would always be there for her.

No more ghosts from the past haunted her, and only the future waited.

A future with Mac.

Epilogue

"Hello, Sullivan."

At that voice—a voice Sullivan heard far too many times in his dreams—his head whipped up. He blinked, sure that he had to be imagining the figure standing in his office doorway. He even shook his head.

She laughed. "No, sorry, you can't blink or even wish me away. I'm here." Celia stepped inside and shut the door.

He rose to his feet. "I wouldn't wish you away." Just the opposite. His voice had sounded too gruff, so he cleared his throat. "Should you…should you be here? You were hurt—"

Celia waved that away. "A flesh wound. I've had worse." Sadness flickered in her eyes. "It's Elizabeth who took the direct hit. I was afraid for a while…but I heard she's better now."

He nodded and crept closer to her. "She's out at the ranch. And I'm sure Mac is about to drive her crazy. I think his protective instincts kicked into overdrive." *So did mine. When I saw you on the floor…*

"I was knocked out for a few moments. My head hit the wall." She shook her head. "The bullet just grazed me."

He hadn't realized that, not at first. He'd just known that she'd been limp in his arms.

A whole lot had sure come into crystal-clear perspective for him in those desperate moments.

"I came to make you a deal."

His head tilted to the side. "A deal?"

"I have information that you want." She pulled a white envelope out of her purse. "I'll give it to you, but you have to promise me one favor."

Suspicious now, he asked, "And just what favor would that be?"

Her smile flashed. A smile that showed off her dimples. Those dimples were so innocently deceptive. So gorgeous.

So Celia.

"You have to agree *before* I tell you what I want." She shrugged. "Sorry, but it's one of those deal-in-the-dark situations. Promise me that you'll be there when I call in this debt. That you'll agree to what I need, and this information is yours."

He wanted to touch her. Needed to kiss her. Instead, he stood there and forced his body to be still. "Just what information is it that you *think* you have?"

"I have your mother's real name."

They had that already. He knew—

"And I have the reason she was put in the Witness Protection Program." She offered the envelope to him. "Do we have a deal? One favor, no questions asked... and you can have her past."

He looked down at the envelope, then he looked back up into Celia's eyes. "Deal."

* * * * *

Read on for an excerpt from
HARD RAIN,
the next installment in
New York Times *bestselling author*
B.J. Daniels's series
THE MONTANA HAMILTONS.

When Brody McTavish sees Harper Hamilton's runaway
horse galloping across the pastures, he does what any
good cowboy would do—gives chase and rescues her.
But they soon have bigger problems when they make a
gruesome discovery—human remains that will dredge
up old Hamilton family mysteries...and bring about a
scandal that could threaten all Harper's loved ones.

CHAPTER ONE

Thunder cracked overhead in a piercing boom that rattled the windows. As she huddled in the darkness, rain pelted down in angry drenching waves. Lightning again lit the sky in a blinding flash that burned in her mind the image before her.

In that instant, she saw him crossing the field carrying the shovel, his head down, rain pouring off his black Stetson. It was done.

Dark clouds blanketed the hillside. Through the driving rain, she watched him come toward her, telling herself she could live with what she'd done. But she feared he could not. And that could be a problem.

BRODY MCTAVISH HEARD the screams only seconds before he heard the roar of hooves headed in his direction. Shoving back his cowboy hat, he looked up from the fence he'd been mending to see a woman on a horse riding at breakneck speed toward him.

Harper Hamilton. He'd heard that she'd recently returned after being away at college. Which meant it could have been years since she'd been on a horse. He was already grabbing for his horse's reins and swinging up in the saddle.

Runaway horse.

He'd been on a runaway horse when he was a kid.

He remembered how terrifying it had been. With that many pounds of horseflesh running at such a deadly speed, he prayed hard she could hang on.

He had to hand it to Harper. She hadn't been unseated. At least not yet.

Harper, yards away on a large bay, screamed. He spurred his horse to catch her and as he raced up beside her, her blue eyes were wide with alarm.

Acting quickly, he looped an arm around her, dragged her off the horse and reined in. His horse came to a stop in a cloud of dust. Her horse kept going, disappearing into the foothill pines ahead.

Brody let Harper slip to the ground next to his horse. The minute her feet touched earth, she started screaming again as if all the wind had been knocked out of her when he'd grabbed her but was back now.

"You're all right," he said, swinging out of the saddle and stepping to her to try to calm her.

She spun on him, leading with her fist, and caught him in the jaw. He staggered back more from surprise than the actual blow, but the woman had a pretty darned good right hook.

He stared at her in confusion. "What the devil was that about?"

Picking up a baseball-sized rock, she brandished it as she took a few steps back from him, all the time glancing around, seeming either to expect more men to come out of the foothills, or looking for a larger weapon.

Had the woman hit her head? He spoke as calmly as he would to a skittish horse—or a crazy woman. "Calm down. I know you're scared. But you're all right now." It had only been a few months since the two of them were attendants at her sister Bo's wedding, not that they hadn't known each other for years.

She peered under the brim of his hat as if only then taking a good look at him. "Brody McTavish?" She stared at him as if in shock. "Have you lost your mind?"

Brody frowned, since this hadn't been the reaction he'd expected. "Ah, correct me if I'm wrong," he said, rubbing his jaw. "But I don't think this is the way most women would react after a man saves her life."

"You think you just saved my life?" Her voice rose in amazement.

"You were *screaming* like either a woman in trouble or one who has lost her senses. I assumed, as any sane person would, that your horse had run away with you. No need to thank me," he said sarcastically.

"*Thank you?* For scaring me half to death?" She dropped the rock and dusted the dirt off her hand onto her jeans. "And for the record, I wasn't *screaming*. I was…expressing myself."

"Expressing yourself at the top of your lungs?"

Harper jammed her hands on her hips and thrust out her adorable chin. He recalled her sister's wedding back at Christmastime. While both attendants, they hadn't shared more than a few words. Nor had he gotten a chance to dance with her. His own fault. He hadn't wanted to get in line with all her young suitors.

"It was a beautiful morning," she said haughtily. "I hadn't been on a horse in a long time and it felt so good that I couldn't resist expressing it." She looked embarrassed but clearly wasn't about to admit it. "Do you have a problem with that?"

"Nope. But when I see a woman riding like a wild person, screaming her head off, I'm going to assume

she's in trouble and needs some help. My mistake."
Didn't she know how dangerous it was riding like that
out here? If her horse had stepped into a gopher hole…
A lecture came to his lips, but he clamped his mouth
shut. "You have a nice day, Miss Hamilton." He tipped
his hat, grabbed up his reins and started to walk back
toward his property.

"You're just going to walk away?" she demanded
to his back.

"Since you aren't in need of *my* help…" he said over
his shoulder.

"I thought you would at least help me retrieve my
horse."

He stopped and mumbled under this breath, "If your
horse has any sense he'll keep going."

"I beg your pardon?"

Brody took a breath and turned to face her again.

Her blond hair shone in the morning sunlight, her
blue eyes wide and filled with devilment. He recalled
the girl she'd been. Feisty was an understatement. While
nothing had changed as far as that went, she was definitely no longer a girl. He would have had to be blind
not to notice the way she filled out her jeans and West-
ern shirt.

She shifted her boots in the dust. "I'd appreciate it
if you would help me find my horse."

"By all means let me help you find your horse then.
As you said, it's the least I can do. Would you care to
ride…*Miss Hamilton*?" He motioned to his horse, glad
he hadn't called her *Princess*, even though it had been
on the tip of his tongue.

Looking chastised, she shook her head. "And, please,
my name is—"

"Harper. I know."

"Glad you didn't mistake me for my twin." She sounded more than a little surprised. "Not even my own father can tell us apart at times."

He could feel her looking at him, studying him like a bug under a microscope. He wondered what she'd majored in at college. Nothing useful, he would bet.

"Thank you for helping me find my horse," she said into the silence that fell between them. "I really don't want to be left out here on foot if my horse has returned to the barn."

He thought the walk might do her some good but was smart enough not to voice it. "The last I saw of your mare she was headed up into the foothills. I would imagine that's where we'll find her, next to the creek."

She glanced up at him. "I apologize for hitting you." When he said nothing, she continued. "With everything that's been going on in my family, I thought you were… Anyway, I'm sorry that I hit you and that I misunderstood your concern." He could hear in her voice how hard that apology was for her.

And, he had to admit, her family had recently definitely been through a lot. The family had seemed to be under attack since her father, Senator Buckmaster Hamilton, had announced he would be running for president. Three of her sisters had been threatened. Not to mention the mother she'd believed dead had returned out of the blue after twenty-two years—and her stepmother had been killed in a car accident. It was as if tragedy was tracking that family.

"Apology accepted," he said as he picked up her cowboy hat from the dust and handed it to her.

As they walked toward sun-bleached cliffs and shimmering green pines, he mentally kicked himself. He'd had a crush on Harper—from a distance, of course—for years, waiting for her to grow up, and now that she finally had and he'd managed to get her attention, he couldn't imagine a worse encounter.

Not that he wasn't knocked to his knees by her crooked smile or the way she had of cocking her head when she was considering something. Not to mention the endless blue of her wide-eyed innocence—all things he'd noticed from the first time he'd laid eyes on her. He smiled to himself, remembering the first time he'd seen her. She'd just been a freckle-faced kid.

Somehow, he'd thought... She'd be grown-up and one day... He told himself someday he and Harper would have a good laugh over this, before he mentally kicked himself.

And to think he thought he'd rescued the woman of his dreams—until she'd hit him.

Brody McTavish. Harper grimaced in embarrassment. She'd been half in love with him as far back as she could remember. Not that he had looked twice at her. He'd been the handsome rowdy teen she used to spy on from a distance. She'd been just a girl, much too young for him. But Brody had come to parties her older sisters had put on at the ranch. She and Cassidy were too young to attend and were always sent up to bed, but Harper often sneaked down when everyone else, including her twin, thought she was asleep.

Several times Brody had caught her watching, and she'd thought for sure he would snitch on her, but he hadn't. Instead, he'd given her a grin and covered for her. Her nine-year-old heart had beat like a jackhammer in her chest at just the thought of that grin.

She'd seen Brody a few times after that, but only in passing. He'd graduated from high school and gone off to college before coming back to the ranch. She'd been busy herself, getting an education, traveling, experiencing life away from Montana. When she'd heard that her sister Bo was dating Jace Calder, she'd wondered if he and Brody were still best friends.

It wasn't until the wedding that she got to see him again. She hadn't been surprised to find that he was still handsome, still had that same self-deprecating grin, still made her now grown-up heart beat a little faster. She'd waited at the wedding reception for him to ask her to dance since they were both attendants, but he hadn't. She'd told herself that he probably still saw her as a child, given the difference in their ages.

Glancing over at him now, she didn't even want to consider what he must think of her after this. Not that she cared, she told herself, lifting her head and pretending it didn't matter. He probably didn't even remember the secret they had shared when she was a girl.

As they walked, though, she couldn't help studying him out of the corner of her eye. Earlier, she hadn't appreciated how strong he was. Now that she knew he wasn't some predator who had been trying to abduct her—something she'd been warned about since she was the daughter of a wealthy rancher and US senator—she took in his muscled body along with the chiseled features of his handsome face in the shade of his straw cowboy hat.

No matter what he said, he hadn't accepted her apology. He was still angry with her. She'd given him her best smile when he'd returned her hat from the ground and all she'd gotten was a grunt. Her smile was all it usually took with most men. But Brody wasn't most men. Wasn't that why she'd never been able to forget him?

"I feel as if we have gotten off on the wrong foot," she said, trying to make amends.

Another grunt without even looking at her.

"My fault entirely," she said, although she didn't really believe that was true and hoped he would agree.

But he said nothing, nor would he even look at her. He was starting to irritate her. She was doing her best to make up for the misunderstanding, but the stubborn man wasn't giving her an inch.

"You can't just keep ignoring me," she snapped, digging in her boot heels as she stopped shy of the pine-covered hillside. "Have you even heard a word I've said? If you don't look at me right this minute, Brody McTavish, I'm going to—"

He swung on her. Had she not been standing flat-footed she would have stumbled back. Instead, she was rooted to the ground as suddenly he was in her face. "I've *been* listening to you and I've *been* looking at you for years," he said, his voice deep and thick with emotion. "I've *been* waiting for you to grow up." His voice faltered as he dropped his horse's reins. "Because I've been wanting to do this since you were sixteen."

Grabbing her, he pulled her against his rock-hard body. His mouth dropped to hers. Her lips parted of their own accord, just as her arms wrapped around his neck. Her heart hammered against her ribs as he deepened the kiss and she heard herself moan.

The sudden high-pitched whinny of a horse only

yards away brought them both out of the kiss in one startled movement. Turning, she could see her horse in the trees. Her first thought was that the mare had gotten into a hunter's snare, because the whinny was one of pain—or alarm.

Brody grabbed her arm as she started past him to see what was wrong with her horse. "I think you should wait here," he said, letting go of her arm as he took off toward the pines.

"My horse—"

"Stay here," he said more sternly over his shoulder.

Still stunned by the kiss and anxious about her horse, she set off after him. The ground was soft under her feet. She saw where fresh soil had washed down through the pines, forming a dark, muddy gully.

Her horse was partway up the hillside near where the rain a few nights ago had loosened the soil and washed it down the hillside. As Brody approached, the mare snorted and crow-hopped away a few feet.

"She's afraid of you," she called to his retreating backside. She could hear him speaking softly to the horse as he approached. She followed, although she was no match for his long legs.

An eerie quiet fell over the hillside as she stepped into the shadowed pines. She slowed, frowning as she finally got a good look at her horse. The mare didn't seem to be hurt and yet Harper had never seen her act like this before.

"I thought I told you to stay back," Brody said as she came up behind him. "You've never been good at following orders, have you?"

So he did remember her sneaking downstairs at her sisters' parties. She felt a bump of excitement at that news, but it was quickly doused. Past him, she saw that her horse's eyes were wild. The mare snorted again, stomped the ground and shied away, to move a few yards back from them and the gully.

"What is wrong with her?" Harper demanded, afraid it was something she had done.

"She's reacting to what the hard rain dislodged and sent down the hillside in an avalanche of mud," Brody snapped. What was he talking about? As she started to step past him to get a look, he put a hand out to stop her. "Harper, you don't want to see this."

She *did* want to see whatever it was and resented him telling her she didn't. Protective was one thing, but the man was being ridiculous. She'd been raised on a ranch. She'd seen her share of dead animals, if that was what it was. She stepped around him, determined to see what the storm had exposed.

At first all she saw were old, grimy, weathered boards that looked like part of a large wooden box. Then she saw what must have been inside the container before it had washed down the slope and broken open.

Her pulse jumped at the sight, her mind telling her she wasn't seeing what her eyes told her she saw. *"What is that?"* she whispered into the already unnerving quiet as she took a step back.

"From the clothing and long hair, I'd say it was the mummified body of a woman who, until recently, had been buried up on that hillside."

*Find out what happens next in
HARD RAIN by* New York Times
*bestselling author B.J. Daniels.
Available now wherever
HQN Books and ebooks are sold.
www.Harlequin.com*

"Hello, Sullivan."

At that low, husky voice—a voice Sullivan had heard far too many times in his dreams—his head whipped up. He blinked, sure that he had to be imagining the figure standing in his office doorway. He even shook his head, as if that small movement could somehow make the woman before him vanish.

Only she didn't vanish.

She laughed, and the small movement made her short red hair brush lightly against her delicate jaw. "No, sorry, you can't blink or even wish me away. I'm here." Celia James stepped inside and shut the door behind her.

He rose to his feet in a quick rush. "I wouldn't wish you away." Just the opposite. His voice had sounded too gruff, so he cleared his throat. He didn't want to scare her away, not when he had such plans for her. *And she's actually here. Close enough to touch.* "Should you... should you be here? You were hurt—"

Celia waved that injury away with a flick of her hand.

"A flesh wound. I've had worse." Sadness flickered in her eyes. "It's Elizabeth who took the direct hit. I was afraid for a while…but I heard she's better now."

He nodded and crept closer to her. Elizabeth Snow was the woman his brother Mac—MacKenzie—intended to marry as fast as humanly possible. Elizabeth was also the woman who'd been shot recently—when she faced off against a killer who'd been determined to put Elizabeth in the ground.

Only Elizabeth hadn't died, and that particular case… it had brought Celia back into Sullivan's life.

Now I can't let her leave.

He schooled his expression as he said, "She's out at the ranch. And I'm sure Mac is about to drive her crazy." He was absolutely certain of that fact. "I think his protective instincts kicked into overdrive." *So did mine. When I saw you on the ground…*

"I came to make you a deal," Celia said as she took a step toward him.

His head tilted to the side as he studied her. "A deal?" Now he was curious. Celia wasn't exactly the type to make deals. She was the type to keep secrets. The type to always get the job done, no matter what.

During Sullivan's very brief stint with the CIA, he'd met the lovely Celia.

And he'd fallen hard for her.

Until I thought she'd betrayed me.

Find out what happens in ALLEGIANCES by New York Times bestselling author Cynthia Eden.

Available May 2016 wherever Harlequin® Intrigue books and ebooks are sold.
www.Harlequin.com

HIEXP0416R

Turn your love of reading into rewards you'll love with
Harlequin My Rewards

Join for FREE today at
www.HarlequinMyRewards.com

Earn **FREE BOOKS** of your choice.

Experience **EXCLUSIVE OFFERS** and contests.

Enjoy **BOOK RECOMMENDATIONS**
selected just for you.

PLUS! Sign up now
and get **500** points
right away!

Earn
FREE
REWARDS
Join
Today!
HarlequinMyRewards.com

MYR16R

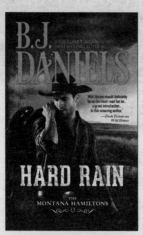

THE WORLD IS BETTER WITH

Romance

Harlequin has everything from contemporary, passionate and heartwarming to suspenseful and inspirational stories.

Whatever your mood, we have a romance just for you!

Connect with us to find your next great read, special offers and more.

⊕ HARLEQUIN®

A *Romance* FOR EVERY MOOD™

HARLEQUIN®

A *Romance* FOR EVERY MOOD™

JUST CAN'T GET ENOUGH?

Join our social communities
and talk to us online.

You will have access to the latest
news on upcoming titles and special
promotions, but most importantly,
you can talk to other fans about your
favorite Harlequin reads.

Harlequin.com/Community

Facebook.com/HarlequinBooks

Twitter.com/HarlequinBooks

Pinterest.com/HarlequinBooks

HSOCIAL